Kara's Journey Through The Realm

Katrina Rayne

"Kara's Journey Through The Realm" is a book which, at first glance, is a fantasy adventure novel, and indeed it is. However, it is much more than that. It is the story of one young woman's physical journey to be reunited with her roots, but it is more importantly a journey of self-discovery. Kara , Shaydon and their friends' battle to defeat Safiri and the Themians is exciting, but I think Kara's journey to realisation of her own worth is even more important. This is a book that will appeal to teenagers, especially girls. I am most certainly not a teenager, and I really enjoyed it and am most anxious to follow more adventures of Kara, Shaydon and their friends. A really, really good read.

May Winton

This paperback edition published 2020 by Jasami Publishing Ltd
an imprint of Jasami Publishing Ltd
Glasgow, Scotland
https://jasamipublishingltd.com

ISBN 978-1-913798-05-5

Visit JasamiPublishingLtd.com to read more about all our books and to purchase them. You will also find features, author information and news of any events, also be the first to hear about our new releases.

Acknowledgements

Illustrator

Marita Morianos

Critical Reader

May Winton

First I want to thank my children, the lights of my life.

George-Aiden you have been my rock through thick and thin, my champion, my sounding board. Thank you for always believing in me, no matter what.

Janna I am grateful to you for your encouragement and belief in my story, for stepping in and managing things whilst I was engrossed in my writing. Thank you especially for the delicious, memorable meals.

Marita, my talented artist, thank you so much for the beautiful illustration, you captured the image I had in my mind perfectly.

Big thank you's must go to Helen and Kieta for your support, suggestions and being there through tough times. You both helped me get this book 'off the ground'.

Kieta the hours you put into reading through the book and providing me with feedback have meant so much.

To Michele, Joy, Paula, Holly and all the behind-the-scene contributors at Jasami Publishing, thank you for providing a wonderful home for my book.

Michele you have been a tremendous support, your continuous enthusiasm and kindness keeps me motivated.

May, thank you for your expertise. Your guidance has been invaluable, helping me to become a better writer.

Thank you to my family and friends who have supported me through this, you know who you are.

Glossary of Terms at the end of novel.

Dedication

For my children, Marita, Janna and George-Aiden
I love you with all my heart and more.

Chapter One

Nightmares and Memories

*T*he dark man drew near, appearing to grow larger with every step. His eyes blazed like red hot coals. He radiated an unbearable heat which scorched the nearby trees. The air was thick and barely breathable. Kara clutched her throat in terror. Tears of fear streamed down her cheeks. She knew what was coming … The man exploded into red angry flames …Kara screamed and fell!

Kara sat on her bedroom floor, trembling and struggling for breath. 'It's just the dream, it's just the dream,' she repeated to herself over and over again, grasping for reality. She tried to remember what her best friend, Shaydon, had told her to do if she should have this nightmare. *"Breathe deeply, imagine a golden white light deep within your core beaming outwards to embrace and shield you."*

The light snapped on and the rotund figure of Maja, Kara's guardian, stood in the doorway.

"What on earth Kara Gabriel?" Maja blurted in agitation. "You're making such a racket you'll wake Dajo up!" Her face softened, however, as she helped Kara up from the floor and tucked her back into bed. She smiled sympathetically at her. "The same nightmare again?"

Kara nodded, her big golden brown eyes blinking back tears.

"Maja, please tell me how you found me again, please." Kara implored. "I know you've told me a thousand times, but it always helps me feel better."

Maja sighed, she could see that Kara would not be able to sleep. It had become somewhat of a routine, Kara would have the same nightmare over and over again and the only way to get her settled was to sit with her and repeat the tale of that fateful mysterious day.

"It was early one foggy morning, was it twelve or thirteen years ago? I can't remember exactly..." Maja rubbed her eyes tiredly as she lay down next to Kara. "I was out in the herb garden when I heard a strange cry coming from the whispering woods nearby...."

Maja and Dajo were a childless couple who lived in a comfortable cottage at the edge of a large forest called Faylin, but to the people who lived nearby, the forest was known as the Whispering Wood because it always sounded like the big old trees were whispering to each other.

Maja was a plump, kindly woman, she always looked rather unkempt from being out in the garden or forest. Wounded forest creatures and birds were drawn to her nurturing nature. She would secretly take them in and tend to them, because she was afraid of upsetting her husband, Dajo, who had expressly forbidden her from bringing 'unwanted' creatures into their home.

Dajo was a tall, strong hardworking man, who always looked well put together, contrasting oddly with his disheveled wife. He was authoritarian and insisted his word be law in his home. He was prone to terrible rages if he felt his authority had been questioned or disobeyed by his wife and foster daughter. He was not an entirely bad man but believed in the old-fashioned notion that women were inferior and could not look after themselves. He had an unusual electrical energy about him which belied his very predictable nature.

Maja remembered being intrigued by the sound of the cry. She tried to ignore it because she was already in enough trouble over a stray cat... but the cry grew even more distressed

Throwing caution to the wind she dropped the herbs. "Come on Bruno, let's go!" she yelled to her large beloved dog. The only pet she was allowed.

Together they set off into the woods following the sound of the cry. Despite the fogginess of the morning, the sun beamed weakly through the branches in dappled patches, Maja felt as if she were jogging through a newly painted watercolour. The fog began to shift as the sun rose higher in the sky. They came upon a small clearing in the wood and under the shelter of an old tree, nestled on a mound of twigs, moss and soft leaves lay a small wriggling bundle. A baby, about a year old, was yelling, kicking and punching frustratedly trying to free herself from the tight swaddling she was wrapped in. Maja immediately picked her up and loosened the swaddling while Bruno sniffed and slobbered excitedly. The baby stopped mid cry to look curiously into Maja's kind brown eyes. Maja's heart melted instantly, and she fell in love with this unusual golden eyed baby girl.

Inside the swaddled blanket Maja discovered a pretty multicoloured crystal bracelet and a small cream envelope. She opened the envelope and there written in an elegant golden scroll were these words.

'Here lies baby Kara Gabriel. I have placed her in your care Maja, because I know you will take her into your home and love her without question. I have taken every precaution to ensure her safety with you. The time will arise one day when she will be called for, to return to her rightful home and you must let her go as easily as I trust you will take her in….'

Before Maja could read the few remaining words, the paper crumbled into gold dust in her hand. The words she had read though, remained forever etched in a special place in her heart.

Maja paused in the memory, eyes misting over, it had seemed like yesterday. Thankfully Dajo had instantly become as enamoured with Kara as she herself had, and accepted her into their home, for once, not questioning Maja's nurturing ways. Maja sat up wearily and gazed down at Kara who had drifted into sleep, her lips curved in a sweet smile.

Kara had grown into a lovely young teenager, she was tall and slender and moved with a quiet gracefulness. She had unusual golden-brown eyes and long dark hair, which was forever falling into her eyes, even when tied back. Her hair was naturally highlighted from all the time she spent in the sun. As much as Kara loved to spend time outside on sunny days either with Shaydon or her two best friends Tawny and Lina, she was happiest when it rained. Her friends would run for shelter, but Kara would play and dance in the rain alone and would return thoroughly refreshed and filled with a positive energy that would last for hours.

Maja shook her head wondering, as she often did, where Kara came from. She leant forward and dropped a gentle kiss on her forehead. She saw that Kara held the crystal bracelet loosely in her hand.

"The day I brought you home," Maja murmured softly, "there was the biggest, brightest rainbow I have ever seen, beautifully arched over our cottage."

"You'll be safe here." Maja whispered as she turned out the lights.

The next day Kara was woken by the sound of raised voices. Maja and Dajo were arguing loudly as usual. They couldn't seem to see eye to eye on anything. Kara sighed and pulled the pillow over her head.

"I don't like it!" Dajo shouted. "How many times have I told you to keep Kara away from him, he is a hippy and too old to be hanging around her. I know it's him who fills her head with foolish notions that will only get her into trouble."

"Shaydon is not a hippy, he is a wonderful, open minded young man!" Maja yelled back. "He has taught

Kara so much, he teaches her things we could never teach her. She needs him in her life...I can't explain it."

"Keep Shaydon away, I don't want to have to tell you again…and you can also stop encouraging her with ideas that she's from another world. I know you think Shaydon is too. Madness! She needs to grow up and eventually settle down with a good man who'll take care of her. You'll stop with these foolish fantasies if you know what's good for her!"

"But the letter…"

"Utter nonsense, you made up a delusional tale all those years ago and now you've come to believe it yourself."

Kara could not bear it any longer. She jumped out of bed and stormed into the kitchen.

"Dajo will you stop it!" she blurted.

Dajo spun round to face her, the air crackled around him. "I will not have your head filled with anymore of this!" He slammed his fist on the table. "You have been meeting up with Shaydon after I expressly forbade it!"

"Shaydon says…"

"I don't give a damn what Shaydon says!" Dajo exploded. "I took you in, fed and clothed you, I raised you, and you think Shaydon knows better than me!" He knocked a chair over angrily.

Kara could feel her own anger battling with her feelings of guilt, Dajo had taken her in after all, but why did he have to be so overbearing and controlling.

"I don't know what you have against Shaydon, and I don't understand why you say Maja and I can't think for ourselves!" She glared at Dajo. "And why do you keep insisting I must settle down with a man who'll take care of me? Maybe I can take care of myself."

"Wake up and face reality before it's too late. A young girl taking care of herself." He scoffed. "You are living in a dream world … women wanting to be independent."

He shook his head. "There's no need for women in the workplace where they just cause confusion and chaos. The sooner you realise this the better. You'll find someone to take care of you after I'm gone, I'll make sure of it!"

The oven buzzer went off just then making them all jump. Maja opened the oven and took out a cheese and bacon quiche. The fragrant aroma had a soothing effect and the tension eased slightly.

Dajo picked up the overturned chair and pushed it back under the table before he walked across the kitchen to Kara, he placed his hands on her shoulders and Kara felt the static in his touch.

He looked into her eyes and spoke gruffly. "I love you Kara and I don't want to see you get hurt. I swore I would protect you from the day I first saw you, but I can't do that if you and Maja go disobeying me behind my back. Don't run around chasing dreams, that can only lead to disappointment and frustration … know your place and you will always be looked after." He pulled her close to him briefly then walked out the back door.

Kara watched through the kitchen window as he walked away. A sadness came upon her, a feeling that she would never see him again and despite all his faults, she did love him. She wondered yet again what he had against

Shaydon. Shaydon was like an older brother and mentor to her.

Her first memory of Shaydon was when she had been about four years old. It had been a pleasant sunny day and Maja had taken her and Bruno out for a picnic in the woods. Maja had fallen asleep under a large tree and Kara had wandered away deep into the forest with Bruno dutifully following behind. Kara remembered feeling afraid as she had got lost in a dark part of the forest. She felt the trees were closing in on her. Bruno had suddenly barked loudly and fiercely and she had burst into startled tears.

"Whoa there, easy now old boy," came a deep soothing voice from behind one of the trees.

A tall, strong looking young man stepped out confidently. He had a handsome, tanned face, his dark brown eyes reflected a natural humour and zest for life. His brown hair fell loosely to his shoulders. He respectfully held his hand out for Bruno to sniff. Bruno sniffed the man's hand tentatively and then barked once to confirm his approval.

Shaydon petted Bruno before he turned to Kara. "What are you doing so far out in the wood little one? Are you lost?"

Between sobs Kara tried to tell him where she lived. Shaydon had comforted her and assured her that he and Bruno would get her safely home. Before long Kara stopped crying. She felt safe with Shaydon and had trusted him implicitly ever since. She remembered him being fascinated with her bracelet and he had asked her if he could examine it more closely. He had looked at it and an expression of wonder had crossed his face, he smiled as he clasped it back on her wrist.

"This is a very special bracelet, little one, take good care of it."

"I like your necklace too." Kara reached to touch the sun shaped locket that hung from the gold chain he wore around his neck.

Shaydon pulled back slightly, a shadow crossed his face briefly as he looked away. Bruno barked again in warning and Shaydon patted him reassuringly before turning smiling eyes back to Kara.

"What is your name little one?"

"Kara Gabriel."

Shaydon's eyebrows raised almost to the top of his forehead. "I knew it." He said to himself.

"Huh?"

"Ummmm... 1 knew that you would have a very important name." Shaydon said rubbing the back of his neck and shoulders. "Because you look like a very special little girl."

He held his hand out to her. "Come along Kara Gabriel, let's take you home."

Kara took his hand willingly and he smiled, "I am so very pleased to meet you Kara, this is a very good day indeed." He called to Bruno. "Lead on old man."

Bruno lead them back to Maja's picnic spot. It was not difficult to find as they heard Maja calling out frantically for Kara and Bruno before they even saw her. Maja had dissolved into a mass of semi hysterical, semi relieved tears when they had appeared and could not thank Shaydon enough, and eventually invited him back to the cottage for tea.

From that day on Shaydon had visited Kara regularly. He encouraged her to learn new things and would often surprise her, sometimes he would show up with a couple of horses and give her riding lessons, other times he would arrive with a sling of bow and arrows and take her into the forest for target practice, he would often gift her beautiful big books filled with adventure and fantasy stories. He keenly encouraged Kara's love of books.

As time passed his visits became less frequent. Between Dajo's attempts to keep Shaydon away and Kara starting at the little local school, their meetings were reduced to one or two afternoons a week. Kara looked forward to their meetings, it was always the highlight of her week. He showed great interest in what she was learning at school and was very proud of her when she told him how she had stood up to the school bullies who had been picking on her tiny friends Tawny and Lina. Kara had been outraged at the bullies and the three friends had taken a stand, putting the bullies firmly in their place. However, she found her recurring nightmare far more frightening than the real-life bullies. Shaydon seemed to be very concerned about her nightmares and always advised her to find an inner light that would protect her when she was in the midst of them.

He had also been a great source of comfort to both her and Maja when their beloved Bruno had died from old age. That was the first time Kara had found herself having to deal with grief.

Shaydon had always encouraged her to be independent and stand up for herself and her friends, but Dajo continually discouraged any female independence at all and Kara grew up conflicted as she valued both of their opinions highly.

When questioned about his occupation Shaydon had said that he was a forest ranger which Dajo thought was a very unlikely job and he forbade Kara to spend any more time with him. Maja adored Shaydon and she knew he was no threat to Kara at all. She always covered up his visits so Dajo was never any the wiser. *Until now,* Kara thought. *I wonder how he found out?*

As if on cue, there was a knock at the front door. Shaydon stood there smiling but looking slightly agitated.

"Hi Kara, please go and get dressed quickly," he said excitedly, not waiting for her response. "Something's happened, something I have been waiting upon for a long time. You need to come with me now, I'll explain on the way. Where's Maja? I must speak with her."

Kara hurriedly got dressed. She wondered what had got Shaydon so excited, it took a lot to rattle his composure. She felt slightly unsettled by the fact that he had come in the morning because he never came to see her in the mornings. "Must be a really big deal," she muttered to herself as she walked quickly towards the kitchen. She slowed down when she heard the tone of their voices and stood by the door looking into the kitchen. Shaydon held Maja in his arms, Maja was crying.

"You knew this day had to come Maja," Shaydon murmured gently, "I have to take Kara to her true home now."

"I know Shaydon, from the moment I met you… I knew you were from the same world as Kara. Please forgive Dajo for trying to keep you away. He means well and has only ever wanted to keep her safe."

Maja looked up and saw Kara at the door. "Come in lovey." She wiped her eyes on her apron.

"What's going on?" Kara asked.

"I'll explain on the way." Shaydon told her again. "We must leave at once as I don't know how long the portal will stay open. It's time for you two to say goodbye. I'll wait for you outside."

He hugged Maja again before leaving the room.

"Oh Kara…" Maja cried "I hoped this day would never come."

She took Kara in her arms and held her tightly.

"I don't understand-"

"Yes, you do." Maja interrupted gently. "Remember the letter that came with you. I always knew someone would come for you… and I had a feeling it would be Shaydon. Don't cry Kara." Maja wiped Kara's tears from her cheeks. "I know you'll be safe with him."

Kara buried her head in Maja's shoulder. "Will I ever see you again?"

"I don't know my child, but we will always be in each other's hearts." She stepped away from Kara. "Go now, before I lock you away and never let you leave."

Kara turned back at the door. "I love you... and I'm so grateful to you and Dajo for taking me in and keeping me safe all these years. Please tell him." She left then, not waiting for a reply.

Chapter Two

Faylin Forest

Shaydon strode ahead of Kara. She followed somewhat reluctantly and kept glancing back. Strands of her hastily tied up hair had loosened and kept falling in her eyes, which were usually golden brown and enhanced by the dappled shades of the forest but that morning they were darkened by her thoughts t and by her apprehension as she watched Shaydon. Shaydon's hair was pulled back from his face and his handsome features were lit up with excitement as he called back to her.

"Come on Kara, I don't know how much time we have." He waited for her to catch up to him.

"You said you would explain on the way." Kara brushed her hair off her face.

"We're going home Kara."

"What do you mean?"

Shaydon paused to look intently at Kara. "You are not from this world Kara, which I suspect you have always known deep down. You and I both come from a much smaller world called The Realm of the Rainbow. Our world is a bridge between this world and other worlds or higher dimensions."

He put up a hand to stop her as she began to interrupt. "There are many such bridges on earth and across the universe, but you'll learn of these in time. A thick veil hides these bridges but sometimes the veil grows thin and the aura of our world can be seen. It looks like a rainbow to the people of earth."

"You are joking." Kara narrowed her eyes.

Shaydon ran his hand along a nearby tree trunk.

"Faylin Forest is the border between the earth and our Realm. You can't deny the mystical charm of these woods." He challenged gently. "Do you remember the time you saw a unicorn here in the forest? You were with Tawny and Lina and they couldn't see it, they thought you were making it up and when the unicorn disappeared you thought that you had imagined the whole thing… well you hadn't imagined it, there *is* a unicorn from our world, trapped here on earth, his name is Mystique."

"Why couldn't Tawny and Lina see it?"

"Because they are not from our world, earthlings have very limited sight. Our Realm is of a higher dimension than earth and so we are able to see the esoteric beings. You'll find all sorts of higher beings and magical creatures on earth's enchanted borders."

"You said the unicorn was trapped here?"

"Speaking of trapped...let's walk and talk."

Shaydon took her arm and began to walk briskly. "You and I have also been trapped here since the portal to our Realm closed suddenly about thirteen years ago, nobody has been able to pass to or from The Realm since...until now...it has mysteriously opened and we don't know how long it will remain open. We have to hurry."

"Why haven't you told me any of this before?" Kara swept a branch out of the way.

"I was trying to protect you."

"That doesn't make any sense."

"Remember when I told you that thoughts emit vibrations and if these vibrations are strong enough they can draw in what you are thinking about?"

"What you think about - you bring about." Kara remembered.

"Yes, but let me start at the beginning." Shaydon rubbed his back and shoulders. "The Rainbow Realm is made up of seven regions. Your father, Lord Eron, is the ruler of the entire Realm and he resides in Eliada, the Capital Region, where you were born. Lord Eron has ruled unchallenged for eons, however, when you were about a year old a rebellion started in the region of Alfsol, where I come from. Alfsol is the Region of Defense."

A frown creased his brow. "A once proud home for many great warriors. These warriors were sworn to protect The Realm... Commander Caine was in charge and he started the uprising by misleading his warriors." Shaydon's fists clenched and lips tightened. "He had a son called Safiri...Safiri is the demon you dream of."

"What!" Kara looked around in alarm. "The demon I dream of is real? He exists?"

"Yes, he is also trapped somewhere here on earth." Shaydon quickened his pace. "Somehow he kidnapped you before he made his escape. My friend Xylia, protector of Faylin, ambushed him with her forest creatures and she managed to free you before he erupted in flames and disappeared. Xylia is a powerful light being and she conjured a charm before leading Maja to you, she then sealed the cottage in a protective shield which has kept Safiri at bay all these years. That and your ignorance of your true heritage have kept you safe."

Kara shook her head confused.

"If I had told you about The Realm you would have obsessed about it, you would have hungered for more and more information which would have caused intense vibrations. These thought vibrations would have drawn the attention of otherworldly creatures, which in turn could have attracted Safiri who has searched in vain for you and obsessed about your whereabouts. You may have unknowingly magnetised him to you." Shaydon explained. "And if I had told you that your nightmares were a real threat, your fearful thoughts might have sent out dark vibrations which risked revealing you, in spite of Xylia's protective charm."

"So, my biggest nightmare has become a reality." Kara looked around again, imagining dark shadows approaching.

"Safiri has always been a real threat. Xylia would not tell me where you were and when I did find you accidentally all those years ago, she made me promise not to tell you the truth...until the right time, which is now." His lips turned up in a half smile.

"Why haven't I met Xylia?"

"Xylia has a distinctive look about her, ethereal, she would have raised your suspicions, she also feared Safiri would have spies, she kept her distance in order to protect you."

"How did you come to be trapped here?"

Shaydon's lips tightened momentarily. "I came after Safiri." His fists clenched again. "He was gone by the time I got here. I searched every inch of Faylin Forest and beyond, but to no avail. When I finally returned, I found the portal had closed."

There was a loud rustle in the branches and leaves above and a beautiful golden eagle flew down and perched on Shaydon's shoulder. His face relaxed.

"Where have you been Aegle? I was worried we may have to leave you behind," he said to the bird as she gently nudged his ear.

Kara was used to the stunning eagle's presence for she often accompanied Shaydon on his visits to Kara, much to Maja's delight. Aegle was a very unusual looking eagle, she had warm golden feathers and dazzling sapphire blue eyes. Kara wondered if she was one of the otherworldly creatures Shaydon had spoken about. She remembered Shaydon had once said that Aegle reminded him of someone very dear to his heart. When Kara had asked who, Shaydon had changed the subject but not before Kara had seen the pain in his eyes.

Kara tried to process what she had just learned, she had many doubts and questions but she had never had reason to distrust Shaydon before. As she walked through the forest, she looked at it from a new perspective. She had always imagined it was enchanted, but had laughed at her own silly notions, Faylin reminded her of one of the forests in her favorite story books back home. She stopped abruptly.

"Shaydon, will I ever see Maja and Dajo again?"

Shaydon smiled compassionately. "I wish I could say yes but I don't know what the future holds."

Kara continued with Shaydon on his path but part of her wanted to run back to the safety and protection of her guardians and their cottage. She wondered if she would still be safe there and what lay ahead in this unknown world. She nearly turned around several times hoping to head back to the familiarity and comfort of the only home she remembered, but she doubted that she would be able to find her way there as she had never before been this deep into the forest.

As they trudged further into the woods, the trees grew thicker and closer, their trunks more gnarled and knotted, the whispering grew louder and a sense of warning and threat crept through the air. Shaydon spoke a few words in a strange sounding language and the whispers calmed as the trees seemed to shift, making their path easier.

"We are entering Xylia's domain which these trees guard, they won't allow us to pass through without giving a password, the password always changes." Shaydon spoke quietly. "Xylia has telepathic powers which you will discover soon enough, she has sensed our arrival and has sent me the password … telepathically. It still unnerves me … the way she gets into my head. She is expecting us."

The trees gradually thinned out allowing more space between them and eventually they came to a line of ancient willows. The trunks appeared to have old wise faces etched into them. The willows gracefully parted their weeping branches to reveal an enchanted garden. A beautiful scent from the diamond white flowers hung in the air. The flowers twinkled and sparkled in the dark green shrubs that bordered the garden. Crystal like orbs with translucent wings floated through the air. One suddenly whizzed at Aegle and landed on her head. Aegle flapped her wings and shook her head in annoyance which sent the orb flying straight at Kara who caught it between both her hands without thinking. She peered closely between her fingers and was amazed to see the orb was actually an exquisite tiny fairy.

A silvery voice drifted across the air. "Come now little ones, is that any way to welcome our guests?"

The translucent form of a woman floated towards them. Xylia's features became more defined as she approached them.

"Welcome Kara Gabriel," she said pulling Kara into a solid embrace, Kara expected the women's arms to pass straight through her like a hologram and was surprised at the firmness of her touch.

"My...you have grown into a beautiful young woman." Xylia released Kara to look at her.

Kara was unnerved by the depth of Xylia's forest green stare that seemed to look into her soul.

"You must release your fears and doubts Kara." Xylia spoke telepathically as she turned to welcome Shaydon and Aegle. Kara shivered as Xylia's words echoed in her mind. She understood why Shaydon found this telepathic power unsettling.

"It pleases me to see you have kept your crystal bracelet." Xylia's gaze swept back to Kara. "I wondered whether I should leave it with you before Maja found you. I see they have looked after you well but unfortunately have tainted you with their own personal and collective beliefs."

"What do you mean by that?" Kara asked defensively.

"Let us sit." Xylia flicked her wrist and some ornate garden chairs and table appeared. The table was set with a pitcher of golden bubbling liquid and three crystal goblets. Xylia served them each a goblet of the honey tasting drink which warmed Kara's stomach and soothed her rattled nerves. Kara watched Xylia closely as she sipped. She had smooth ethereal ageless features, her hair fell in a mist of silver waves, but the true indication that she may be an ancient being was in the age old wisdom that lingered in the depths of her forest green eyes.

"I mean no offence to you Kara, nor to your guardians, but you have some concerns about returning to your rightful home." Xylia spoke. "Part of you wishes to stay in the home you grew up in… but you can no longer grow there Kara, you cannot be who you are meant to be should you return there. Your guardians have misguided beliefs which are harmful… but reflect the thoughts of many humans. Dajo has an outdated belief that women are inferior and are unable to take care of themselves, and Maja has compounded this belief by seeing herself as a helpless victim. Their opinions and beliefs have seeped into your consciousness."

Xylia gazed into Kara's golden-brown eyes. "It is time to discover your true self on your journey home, my wish is for you to discover your strength and self-worth Kara Gabriel, for it matters not if we can see how strong and worthy you are, if you do not see it yourself."

Aegle took this moment to gently peck at Kara's crystal bracelet.

Shaydon stroked Aegle's feathers. "The different coloured crystals on your bracelet represent the different regions within The Realm. We will have to pass through each region before you reach Eliada."

Kara bit her lip. "It's true, I don't know if I want to go to The Realm. I don't know if I can do it. I am sort of happy at the cottage with Maja and Dajo. What if Safiri follows us to The Realm and destroys us?" She turned to Xylia with pleading eyes. "Xylia you can protect me here."

"Be strong Kara, return to The Realm, you will no longer be safe here." Xylia replied sadly.

"You are brave and loyal Kara." Shaydon spoke. "These are admirable qualities. You have always defended your friends loyally. It takes courage to stand up to bullies as I have seen you do… and you will have the courage to take on Safiri when the time comes, I believe in you and I will be there with you. You have my word."

Kara's eyes glistened. "Thank you," she whispered with uncertainty.

There was a rustle and movement in the nearby shrubbery as a strange looking little man dressed in green and brown crawled out.

"Fergus!" exclaimed Shaydon leaping up.

The two men grasped hands and clapped each other's backs. The odd little man stepped back and glared up at Shaydon. "Ahhh, is it not yerself, young Shaydon. Wasn't I sure we'd not be meeting again!"

"It's so very good to see you Fergus!" Shaydon beamed. "Have you been in The Realm all these years?"

Fergus ignored the question as his beady eyes fell on Kara. "And who have we here?" He eyed her up and down curiously.

"It is my honour to introduce Kara Gabriel." Shaydon said proudly. "Kara this is Fergus, Keeper of the Gate."

Kara reached out to shake Fergus's hand but he stepped back, looking suspiciously from Shaydon to Xylia. "Kara Gabriel? How is this now? Are ye sure?...Are ye sure?" he repeated.

Shaydon and Xylia nodded. Fergus composed a smile. "Well there she is sure and doesn't she have bright eyes on her."

He took her hand and kissed it. "It'd be my pleasure to be meetin' ye, however I'd best be on me way sure now. Must be keepin' that portal open for ye."

Kara resisted the urge to wipe the back of her hand.

"Is the portal safe Fergus? Should we leave immediately?" Shaydon asked.

"No, no... ye have some time... finish up yer business with Xylia." Fergus bounded off calling out, "The Realm is strong!" before he disappeared into the shrubbery.

Shaydon stared after him frowning. "He seems different, where has he been all these years?"

"Fergus is one of the rare few who is able to hide his mind from me." Xylia answered thoughtfully. "We spoke together earlier this morning. He briefly told me his version of the fateful events. A great army appeared at the portal all those years ago. There were Dark Ones who overpowered him, while another foul race stole his Gate Keeper powers before blasting him away to the other side of the earth. Apparently, it has taken him all these years to recover his powers and return to his place of duty."

They heard a noise behind them and they turned to see a beautiful white unicorn walking through the ancient willow trees.

"There you are Mystique." Xylia drifted happily across the garden to the unicorn. "I believe you two have met before, Kara." She smiled back. "Isn't he spectacular?"

Kara's mouth dropped open in awe. She stood in shock as the unicorn approached her and bowed his majestic head. She tentatively reached up to stroke the unicorn's strong sleek neck.

"So you are real after all." She whispered. "How beautiful you are."

Xylia conjured up a bowl of golden apples for Mystique before she returned to her seat and beckoned Kara and Shaydon back to the table. "I have more news from The Realm which I must share with you before you leave."

Shaydon leaned forward expectantly and his golden sun locket slipped out from his shirt. Aegle pecked at it in excitement. Kara had noticed that the eagle always became agitated whenever she saw the locket. Shaydon placed her gently on the grass beside him.

"Tell us." He said to Xylia.

"These past thirteen years we have believed that Commander Caine orchestrated the invasion, but we were all wrong. He was framed by his wife Narcissa." Xylia began. "Somehow Narcissa had obtained a powerful mask with the power of impersonation which she used to impersonate her husband. We have learned that she poisoned him and left him hidden to die alone as she took on his persona. Commander Caine's body was found shortly after the shutdown of the main portal and it was taken to Onain, Region of Visions, to be read. There it was discovered that Narcissa had been trying to convince her husband to start a rebellion for many years. She grew tired of him, thinking him weak and unable to satisfy her desires, so she took matters into her own hands. She wanted The Realm for herself, she wished to overthrow Lord Eron. Commander Caine was completely seduced by his wife but did not view her as a real threat so he did not expose her treachery. Narcissa was a beautiful, seductively powerful women and many men could not resist her. She was Commander Caine's greatest weakness... but his pledge and loyalty to The Realm remained strong until his demise."

Xylia paused to sip from her goblet. "Under the guise of her husband, Narcissa instructed the Alfsol army to go to a remote part of The Realm in the pretence that there was an attack taking place. This was a decoy, leaving the higher regions exposed and vulnerable, which gave her invading army free passage through the lower regions."

Xylia looked to Shaydon. "You will remember your father Aldridge was suspicious of this instruction and he took a small group of men on a different route, you followed your father and know how you came to discover the whereabouts of the real invasion, but you and your father were mistaken in the belief that it was Caine who commanded the invasion, when in fact it was Narcissa… "

Xylia turned back to Kara. "Upon discovery of the deception, Aldridge was then charged with the mammoth task of convincing the Alfsol army to turn around and disobey their Commander, no easy feat, but convince them he did and they saved The Realm, for the most part." Xylia smiled back at Shaydon sadly.

Shaydon's eyes shone. "How are my parents Xylia?"

"Your father has taken leadership of Alfsol and has been the Commander ever since, a worthy and honourable leader." Xylia lay her hand on top of Shaydon's hand. "I fear your mother was struck down at the news of your sister's passing and your disappearance, she has lain in a deep sleep these past years, unable to wake. She lies in Evergreen under the watchful care of The Sage."

Shaydon's shoulders slumped and his head dropped onto his arms, he trembled briefly. Kara stiffened in shock for she did not know that Shaydon had a sister. She watched as Aegle lay her head on Shaydon's shoulder, her dazzling eyes glistening with moisture. Kara turned to Xylia in disbelief.

Xylia rested her hand on Shaydon's back while she spoke telepathically to Kara. *"Shaydon has not told you of his sister Alyne as her passing caused him devastating grief. He will not speak of her to anyone. He came here to find Safiri and avenge his sister."*

Shaydon lifted his head, his eyes were red and his voice cracked. "My mother is not dead, she is asleep."

"It has been many years-"

"She is asleep." Shaydon insisted. "What became of Narcissa?"

"Narcissa has been imprisoned in The Purge." Xylia said before turning to Kara. "The Purge is a prison between The Realm and other worlds. Only Lord Eron has the power to free the souls who are detained there. It is a dark and dismal place of endless bleakness."

Kara looked at Shaydon. "I am so sorry Shaydon, I am so sorry about your sister and your mother...why-"

"My mother sleeps, she will wake again." Shaydon interrupted through tight lips.

Kara stroked Shaydon's arm sadly. She wished she could ease his pain. Her thoughts turned to Safiri.

"You are wondering what Safiri's part is in all of this." Xylia read her mind.

"Narcissa was a cruel heartless mother. Safiri grew up longing for her love. He convinced himself that if he could help her with her evil plans, she would eventually learn to love him and include him in her life. The mask that Narcissa used can only be worn temporarily before the effects wear off, so when she was done impersonating Caine, Safiri took the mask. It soon became evident that her plans had been thwarted. Safiri then used the mask to disguise himself as one of your nursemaids and somehow got into Eliada at rapid speed. Once there, he took you and headed for earth, intending to keep you hostage."

Xylia looked briefly across the garden at Mystique. "I became aware of his intentions and ambushed him here in Faylin, we managed to rescue you before he escaped. In recent years there have been growing whispers between the trees and the forest creatures, rumours of Safiri forming a darker more powerful army than his mother's. He too has been waiting for the portal to open."

"Was Safiri not close to his father?"

"No, another mistake Commander Caine made... although he was a brilliant Commander and ultimately true to The Realm, he was busy and somewhat vain, he enjoyed the glory and status of his position a little too much, making him oblivious to how Safiri was growing up."

Xylia sighed. "Sadly, although he wasn't cruel to Safiri, he was neglectful of him and sometimes indifference and neglect can be just as damaging as outright cruelty."

They all sat in silence for several moments. Xylia cocked her head as if listening for something. The sky darkened. Mystique neighed deeply. The air around them chilled. The whispers from the wood grew louder and became frenzied. They heard axes chopping and branches snapping in the distance and the loud sound of a roaring, crackling fire approaching.

Xylia sprung up, a fierce look in her eyes, spears materialised in both her hands.

"Go Shaydon! Get Kara to the portal... now!" she commanded before vanishing into thin air.

Chapter Three

Sanguinavia

"Hurry Kara!" Shaydon pulled her behind him, frantically pushing through the shrubbery with his other arm.

Darkness lay beyond the garden and Kara's feet seemed to be sinking further into the ground with every step. She felt like they were trying to run blindly through quicksand, bumping into hard trees as they moved. Shaydon held tightly onto her hand but they were sinking fast and were ankle deep in the boggy ground. Just when she thought it was all over a forceful gust of wind picked them up and pushed them through the rest of the forest into a small meadow just beyond. As dark as the forest had been moments before, the meadow, by contrast, was bathed in a light mist of soft swirling colours.

Fergus stood on a hillock in the middle of the magical meadow, waving and calling to them. "Hurry up now Shaydon, the winds are changing!"

Shaydon pulled Kara towards the hillock as an opening appeared in its centre. Kara tried to catch her breath.

Fergus was still yelling. "Jump in quick now, The Realm is strong… go well!"

Shaydon let go of her hand and ducked behind her to push her through the hillock's opening, she fell forward and cried out as she realised there was no ground beneath her feet and dropped down, down... free falling to what she was sure to be her death. Gradually she became aware that she was no longer falling, she was floating, in a swirl of rainbow colours. She heard Shaydon calling her name. He must have jumped in behind her. Eventually her feet lightly touched ground and she staggered slightly as she gained her balance.

"Nice landing." Shaydon beamed as he landed next to her. "You're a natural."

Kara glared at him and pushed him hard, making him fall on his backside. "Thanks for the warning, I thought I was going to die!"

Shaydon lay on his back with a huge grin on his face. "Ahhhh." he inhaled and exhaled deeply before scooping up some dirt from the ground and letting it trickle between his fingers. "It feels so good to be home."

He got up and brushed off his clothes. "I'm sorry Kara, I needed to get you through the portal immediately. I'm sure the darkness in Faylin was caused by Safiri."

Kara looked around in alarm. "Will he follow us down here?"

"He won't be able to get past Xylia and her forest creatures that easily, she is formidable." Shaydon said with awe. "And then he will have to get past the Keeper of the Gate, the portal won't open without a keeper present and Fergus has the ability to disappear at will. If you can't find the keeper, you can't enter."

"The enemy got past Fergus before."

"None of us were expecting an attack before. Now that the portal has opened The Realm will be on high alert, I suspect Fergus was expecting trouble when we entered the meadow and he was just waiting to give us passage. I'm confident he would have disappeared as soon as we passed, thereby blocking the entrance."

"Where are we?" Kara asked looking around feeling a mixture of relief, angst and curiosity. They were in another old worldly forest which was bathed in a deep red aura.

"We are in Sanguinavia, foundation of the Rainbow Realm."

The trees were gnarled, slim and very tall. The earth began to tremble and Kara looked around to see a giant tree approaching them. She could scarcely believe her eyes.

"That's not a tree, it's a Thendron." Shaydon explained quietly. "Thendra are ancient beings who guard the entrance to The Realm, often mistaken for trees."

"Ahh Thorn… aren't you a sight for sore eyes." Shaydon called out in greeting as he set forward to meet the Thendron.

"You are most truly welcome young Shaydon." The treelike creature had a deep rough gravelly voice. It spoke and moved slowly and awkwardly. Kara stumbled backwards as Thorn looked down on her.

"You've nothing to fear Kara." Shaydon caught her. "This is Thorn, one of our beloved Thendra."

"It is an honour to meet you Kara Gabriel." said Thorn reaching out a thin branch like limb.

"Err… my pleasure." mumbled Kara unsure whether to shake the proffered branch or not.

Thorn briefly rested his branch on her shoulder. "Xylia was here earlier, she told me to expect you." He turned to

Shaydon. "We have swapped brief accounts of both our worlds… I trust she has thusly informed you?"

"Yes." Shaydon lowered his eyes. "These past years have felt like centuries, I've longed for home every single day, I wondered if I would ever see it again. I'm so grateful for Kara and Xylia, they made my days bearable and gave me hope that the portal would open."

"You have all been greatly missed." Thorn began to walk away in his awkward manner, beckoning to them. "Come, you must be weary. The red dwarves will be delighted to have you as their honoured guests. You can rest with them this evening."

"Who are the red dwarves?" Kara asked following Shaydon and Thorn.

"The red dwarves are the hardest workers in The Realm." said Thorn proudly. "They farm the fields and provide produce for the rest of the regions. They mine precious gems and metals. They forge the armour and weapons for Alfsol. They build the fountains for Onain. The entire Realm depends on Sanguinavia."

The three companions walked out of the forest into a large field of poppies.

"We have poppy fields like this in Alfsol" Shaydon said as they walked through the calming field. "But Alfsol is known as the home of sunflowers and flame lilies which grow abundantly there."

The stars were starting to appear in the red sky. The moon and the stars seemed closer and much larger than on earth. They came to a winding cobbled path which they followed until they reached a large red brick building. Soft lamp light glowed from the windows.

"You will rest here at Master Lukey's manor," said Thorn.

Two stout dwarves guarded the double front doors of the manor. They grinned and saluted the trio as they approached. Aegle suddenly arrived and perched gracefully on Shaydon's shoulder.

"Good evening friends." Thorn greeted the guards. "I announce the arrival of Lady Kara and Colonel Shaydon. Please escort them to Master Lukey, he is expecting them."

He turned to Kara and Shaydon. "This is where I leave you, unfortunately I cannot fit comfortably through these doors, as you can see. I must, in any case, hasten back to my post at the Red Wood." He bowed awkwardly before he left.

The dwarf guards welcomed them and led them through the doors into a warm great hall. The delicious aroma of roast meat filled the air and Kara's mouth immediately began to water. Shaydon's stomach rumbled in response.

"Greetings most honoured guests!" A large voice boomed from across the hall, where a male dwarf sat on a big wooden throne. He had bright red hair and a long red beard. Cheerful blue eyes twinkled beneath bushy brows.

"Master Lukey!" Shaydon strode across the hall as Lukey rose to meet them. Lukey was rather big for a dwarf. He reached Shaydon's chest in height. They met with a gruff embrace and thumped each other's backs heartily.

The hall had many fireplaces burning with long low tables set throughout the room, the tables and benches were filled with jovial looking dwarves. The celebratory atmosphere was infectious and Kara grinned around at the welcoming faces.

"My dear Lady Kara." Lukey walked up to her. "It is a glad, glad day to see you here. I am Lukey, Steward of Sanguinavia. Please, please make yourself welcome, my home is your home," he gestured around with both arms before embracing her gruffly. "Your father will be so very happy, so very happy indeed." He choked back emotional tears. "It is truly a blessed day to be among the first to witness your return."

He turned her wrist gently to admire her crystal bracelet before he looked back to Shaydon. "Shaydon my good, good man! Come, come both of you! You shall dine with me at my table."

He led them to the largest table at the head of the hall and pulled out a seat next to his for Kara. There were jugs of red Sanguinavian wine, mead and water set along the table and as they sat rustic platters of different roast and stewed meats and root vegetables were laid before them on the table. A good hearty meal was just what they needed. Both Kara and Shaydon tucked into the food straight away and ate their fill. Eventually Kara sat back dreamily in her chair and listened to Shaydon and Lukey's conversation. They spoke of the rebellion and the effects on the different regions but Shaydon would not allow Lukey to linger on the subject of his mother and sister. Kara found it difficult to keep her eyes open. Thoughts of her father floated in and out of her mind, she shook herself awake and wiped some dribble from her chin.

"It is a pity, a pity she has to pass through all of the regions before she meets with Eron." Lukey said in a hushed voice.

"Why?" Kara asked and the men looked surprised to see her awake.

"It's the way of things here Kara." Shaydon answered, "It's not really a rite of passage per se... but on returning to The Realm after being away, it is traditional for each individual to pass through every region before they return home. It's thought to restore harmony and balance within us, which may have faltered whilst away from The Realm. It is an important passage, but don't worry you'll reach home sooner rather than later. Thereafter you can move freely between the regions."

"Will my father meet me along the way?"

"Alas, alas you must complete your journey through the regions first." Lukey pushed his plate aside and leaned forward. "It is the way of things here as Shaydon told you."

He poured Kara a glass of Sanguinavian wine. "A last drink before you sleep, do not worry Kara, you will be reunited with your father soon, soon. I truly, truly hope your journey will be blessed with speed and ease." He clinked glasses with Kara and Shaydon before downing his own drink.

A short while later a sweet little lady dwarf showed Kara to her room. It was simply furnished with a firm bed and a comforting warm hearth. Kara washed quickly before she fell on the bed.

Kara dreamt of talking trees, diamond flowers, poppy fields and riding a unicorn while she floated through swirling misty colours. The unicorn and colours disappeared as she dropped into darkness and landed on hard ground. She heard a crackling noise behind her, slowly she looked around and saw Safiri approaching her, his blazing eyes boring into her. Kara stood up feeling fear but something else too, a small warming glow in the centre of her stomach. She allowed this warmth to grow and fill her up until an empowering light beamed from her in all directions. Safiri stopped in his tracks.

"Feeling brave are you Kara?" he asked in a cruel hard voice. "You weak, useless girl." He laughed derisively. "Do you not know who I am?"

His words stung but Kara lifted her chin defiantly and continued to stand her ground, fists clenched.

"Do you really think you have any power at all? Especially over me? A more useless creature I have never seen." His cruel voice raised slightly as he expanded but he did not draw nearer. "I shan't kill you just yet though, you may still serve a purpose."

Kara looked at him levelly. "Why are you here Safiri?"

Safiri's eyes sparked." You will find out soon enough." He took a step closer. "You won't be strong enough to survive in the end. Not without your father or Shaydon to protect you. Your life will crumble."

"And yet I have survived you before." Kara glared at him. "You can't harm me. You may have taken me from my home but now I'm back and you are not welcome here. You failed before and you will fail again."

Safiri exploded into flames.

Kara stepped back but did not scream. She felt protected by the aura of white light beaming from within her. She could see his figure in the flames as he drew a sword before charging towards her. She dodged aside and swerved behind him, he swung around, his sword raised. A voice within her spoke urgently. *Call for rain, you have the power to call for rain. Rain will stop him!*

"Rain, send rain!" She called out loud and the heavens opened with gusto, pelting rain down upon them… And then, she woke up drenched with sweat, to find herself in the simple bedroom in Lukey's manor.

Once Kara realised it was just a dream she smiled widely. She felt more empowered than ever because she had never confronted Safiri in a nightmare before. *I am home, I am strong, I will survive.* She affirmed to herself.

Later that morning at breakfast Kara told Shaydon and Lukey of her dream.

"This is great progress Kara." Shaydon looked happy and rested. "It's the first time you've confronted Safiri in a dream, your strength and confidence grow."

"You are on home ground, home ground is where your strength lies." Lukey put down his spoon, clapped his hands and a couple of dwarves appeared carrying armour and weapons. "With home ground beneath your feet dear Kara, you are ready to face your fears, face your fears indeed, and we have crafted the perfect gifts for the occasion."

He took a beautifully designed chest plate and an elaborately forged sword from one of the dwarves. "Please, please accept these gifts from the people of Sanguinavia." He stood up to formally present the gifts to Kara.

"These are beautiful! Thank you." she gasped.

With some help from the dwarves Kara put on the chest plate and picked up the sword. She strode confidently to the centre of the hall and swung the sword around.

"It feels so light but powerful at the same time."

She grinned before she tripped over the sword, and blushed as she got up, to the amusement of Shaydon and Lukey. A large purple amethyst had been set in the hilt of her sword and another amethyst had been set in the centre of her chest plate.

"The amethyst is a symbol of your birthplace, Eliada." Lukey walked around her admiringly. "The armour fits you perfectly, wonderful, wonderful!" He turned back to Shaydon, "and you my friend will be in need of these, you surely will."

He took another piece of armour, helmet and sword from the second dwarf and handed them to Shaydon. Kara noticed that these pieces were embedded with beautiful yellow citrine crystals.

"Thank you, my good man, these are perfect." Shaydon grabbed Lukey's hand and clapped him on the back before he eagerly tried on the armour and unsheathed the striking sword,

"I think our first sword fighting lesson is in order," he called to Kara.

They hurried out into the courtyard followed excitedly by several dwarves. Shaydon first showed Kara how to defend herself with simple blocks and parries and how to stand her ground posture centred to keep her balance. There were shouts of well-meaning but often conflicting advice from the onlooking dwarves and soon Kara grew weary. Sword fighting was hard work. They stopped for refreshments.

While they rested Shaydon announced it was time out for the region of Arencia. A group of worried looking dwarves hurried up to Lukey and whispered urgently in his ear.

"This is very, very unusual." Lukey looked confused, scratching his beard. "Unfortunately, my friends, I cannot stay to see you off. I must go immediately, immediately to the mines as there has been an outbreak of fights. This has never, never happened before."

"I'll come with you." said Shaydon.

"No, no." Lukey refused. "It is best you get going, Kara needs to get home as soon as possible, please, please, be on your way."

He stood up abruptly, his bushy face marred with concern and annoyance, and hurried after the dwarves. "Go well!" He called back to them.

Chapter Four

Arencia

Within a short while Kara found herself being accompanied by Shaydon and Thorn as they made their way to the next region, Arencia. Aegle flew ahead of them.

Kara watched her soar near to the clouds and wondered why it was so difficult for Shaydon to speak of his mother and sister. Shaydon and Thorn were deep in conversation. They spoke of The Realm and speculated on the cause of the violent outbreaks in the dwarf mines. They discussed Safiri at length. Kara noticed the red aura of Sanguinavia had faded and a distinct citrus aroma filled the air. As they walked on the colours around them become more intense. Brilliant greens flourished on the grounds and surroundings while a clear azure sky shimmered above. Soft breezes caressed their skin and Kara felt a vitality, that she had not known before, emerge from deep within.

"All is well with the sisters." Shaydon mused

"It would seem so." Thorn agreed.

Kara raised an eyebrow at Shaydon.

"Arencia is governed by two sisters, Aurora and Melia." Shaydon explained. "They both have intensely passionate natures and their moods can have an adverse effect on the weather and skies around them."

"Although their moods may be disturbing at times, they are fair princesses for the most part." Thorn spoke in his awkward gravelly manner. "Fortunately, Aurora is somewhat more grounded than Melia and will usually calm situations before much harm is done."

"Sounds intense." Kara pushed the hair out of her eyes.

"It can be." said Shaydon. "Arencia is known as the Region of Pleasure. Sounds good right? But too much of a good thing has its own set of troubles."

The atmosphere around them had mellowed into a soft orange peachy sunset. They walked over a bridge crossing a babbling brook. Beautiful bird songs filled the air and they breathed in a mixture of citrus and floral aromas. Everything seemed sharper and clearer on the other side of the bridge and Kara's skin began to prickle from the slightly overwhelming sensations. Thorn led them through an orange grove where the citrus scent became even more intense Pretty little white flowers shone like diamonds on the fruit trees reminding her of Xylia's glade, but these appeared altogether brighter, plump juicy oranges seemed to beckon them from the dark green foliage. Thorn murmured a few strange words which sounded similar to the language Shaydon had spoken in Faylin Forest the day before. Kara could hardly believe that it had only been a day since she had left the safe familiarity of the cottage. It felt much longer.

Thorn gestured to the heavily laden branches. "The orange trees of Arencia are most pleased that both of you have returned safely. They offer you their fruits for refreshments."

The oranges almost fell from the branches as Kara and Shaydon plucked them. They peeled open easily and Kara closed her eyes as she bit into an orange segment, the sweet fresh juice burst into her mouth. It was the sweetest orange she had ever tasted.

Shaydon watched her with a knowing smile. "There's nothing quite like the flavours of Arencia."

At the edge of the orange grove stood a large white pavilion inside which a dozen handsome young guards lounged around on comfortable couches.. A couple of them were playing cards. They jumped to attention as Thorn, Shaydon and Kara approached.

"Shaydon?"

"Is that you?"

The young men ran over and Shaydon disappeared under their embraces, back slapping and guffaws....

"We heard you had come back!"

Shaydon held his hands up in mock surrender and laughed at the guards' exuberance. "Look at you all grown up, I wouldn't recognise any of you young fools if it weren't for your bad manners!"

He grabbed one of them in a headlock and rustled his hair. The rest of the guards wrestled Shaydon to the ground bellowing in delight.

Kara raised her eyebrows and bit her lip nervously.

"Some of the young boys of Arencia are sent to Alfsol for guard training. Shaydon mentored these young men before he left." Thorn explained. "Ahem!" He coughed loudly, putting a stop to the raucous reunion.

The guards helped Shaydon up and stood to attention. Shaydon brushed himself off and walked over to Kara, placing a protective hand on her arm.

"You scoundrels are honoured to be in the company of Lady Kara Gabriel," he announced.

The guards' mouths dropped open in surprise but they quickly recovered and each bowed before her and kissed her hand. Kara flushed deeply. She was not used to the attention of such handsome young men. They stared at her in open admiration, looking her up and down, a few of them nudged each other, commenting in undertones.

"Lady Kara please forgive our inappropriate behaviour." The young captain of the guards introduced himself. "We were only boys when the portal closed and you were taken from The Realm. We stand before you in awe and can barely hide our excitement in welcoming you and Colonel Shaydon home."

"Watch out for the lads of Arencia Kara." Shaydon winked. "They can't help themselves; their sweet talk is legendary."

"I would like a word with you young men," Thorn said sternly. "Before I return to my post it seems you need to be reminded of the sanctity and honour of guarding a region's boarders and the befitting manner in which you should present yourselves as guardians!"

Shaydon grinned. "Thank you for bringing us this far Thorn. Kara and I will make our way from here."

He saluted the group of guards. "Good luck."

Kara and Shaydon walked on through bountiful gardens bursting with flowers and fruits. All of Kara's senses seemed to be heightened in this beautiful region. Her taste, touch, hearing and smell were honed beyond anything she had ever experienced before.

She could hear the relaxing sounds of a waterfall nearby and inhaled the intoxicating scents of the vividly coloured flowers which grew everywhere in abundance. She also detected some herbs and spicy notes lingering in the aromas and commented on this.

Shaydon picked a brilliant red flower, breathing in the scent before handing it to Kara.

"Sanguinavia is the foundation of our Realm and most of the produce comes from there. We depend on Sanguinavia for our basic needs," he bent to examine another flower, "but Arencia brings flavour and passion to The Realm, everything in Arencia is sweeter and sharper. Spices and herbs enhance the food here, taking dining to another level. You will find tastes here that you've never experienced elsewhere. It's not just our pallets which are enhanced but all of our other senses as well. I'm sure you've noticed."

They approached three well-manicured paths and Shaydon gestured to the left. "We'll walk by the lake. In Arencia we learn that pleasure is necessary for the soul... but we have to balance it out. For example, a common belief is that if a little of a good thing feels nice, then a lot of that good thing must feel even better. Unfortunately, when it comes to our senses, this does not apply. Excess indulgence can lead to addiction which is enslaving. Being obsessed with chasing temporary pleasures is not a fulfilling way to live and may lead to desperation and depression."

Shaydon smiled sadly. "I sound just like my parents. They gave Alyne and I the same lecture, word for word, about the importance of freedom and balance whenever we visited Arencia."

They walked on in silence for a while before Shaydon spoke again.

"There's a tendency for emotions to blow up here, due to the nature of this region. So, pay attention to your emotions and remember... unpleasant feelings let us know that we need comfort and rebalancing." He sighed heavily. "How I've missed my mother and father."

"I'd love to hear more about your family." Kara took Shaydon's hand and squeezed it, but Shaydon said no more.

The breathtaking golden lake lay before them with the giant peach like sun setting upon it. Kara had never seen such a stunning pink and coppery sunset before. They walked along the lake side by side in companionable silence, appreciating the tranquil beauty.

They were not alone, there were several artists standing behind easels, attempting to capture the essence of the sunset. Couples embraced each other lovingly, enjoying the magical romance of the lake. Nobody paid them any attention as they passed by, everyone was caught up in their own moments.

Eventually Shaydon led her away from the lake's sandy shore up onto lush green grass. In the distance a large shimmering palace bathed in the glow of the orange sunset. They entered the palace gardens where they found families and children playing. Some people sat around the edge of the moat which surrounded it and fed the black and white swans who floated gracefully on the glassy water. A grand ornate bridge crossed the moat. A couple of handsome guards stood on duty. Kara wondered if it was a prerequisite for all guards to be handsome in Arencia.

The guards bowed as they approached. "Welcome Colonel Shaydon and Lady Kara. Our princesses have been waiting in anticipation. They are expecting you."

As soon as the guard finished addressing them, his companion blew an elaborately designed horn and a finely dressed lady appeared on the other side of the bridge. She came across to greet them, curtsying on approach. Kara felt a twinge of apprehension, everything was so grand and well-kept in Arencia and she was still wearing the dusty jeans and T-shirt that she had left home in. She self-consciously tried to smooth down her hair. They followed the lady into the palace which was elegantly decorated and furnished, with beautiful floral arrangements throughout. Stunning artwork graced the walls and a delicious aroma wafted through the palace. The lady showed them into the throne room and there sat upon two golden thrones were the princess sisters; Aurora and Melia. Aurora had long dark chocolate brown hair and an exquisite heart shaped face. Long sweeping lashes framed her dark almond eyes. She was tall and slender. Melia on the other hand was shorter and curvaceous with flaming red hair and mischievous flashing blue eyes. Both princesses stood as Kara and Shaydon approached and then without warning Melia burst into wild laughter and ran across the room into Shaydon's surprised arms, nearly knocking him off his feet. Aurora followed Melia with a warm smile and kissed Shaydon on both cheeks.

Shaydon blushed as Melia fawned over him. "Shaydon we have missed you so very, very much." She ran her hands along his chest.

Aurora turned to Kara. "Welcome home Lady Kara, you won't remember me, but I remember you very well, you were such a beautiful baby and I am pleased to see that your beauty has flourished." She embraced Kara warmly. She smelt of exotic spices and flowers.

"I am most eager to get to know you. People from Eliada are always so knowledgeable and interesting… you must have lots to share from your experiences on earth."

Kara did not feel very knowledgeable or interesting at all and was not sure how to respond.

"Welcome Kara," Melia tore her eyes away from Shaydon.

"Thank you, um, nice to meet you both," Kara smiled nervously.

"We have arranged an awesome banquet to celebrate your return, it will be a party to be remembered!" Melia clapped her hands excitedly. "It has been quite dull here of late," she batted her eyelashes at Shaydon.

"You must be weary from your travels and in need of a refreshing hot bath," Aurora looked them up and down. "Our ladies in waiting will arrange a change of clothes for you."

She clicked her fingers and another fine lady appeared and took Kara and Shaydon to the guest wing of the palace. There were some maids waiting for them and Kara was taken into a beautiful pink and white cloud like room with a large comfortable four poster bed set invitingly in the centre. There was an en-suite marble bathroom with an ornate white and gold bathtub. Kara dropped wearily onto one of the armchairs and pulled off her grubby sneakers while a jasmine and lavender scented bath was prepared for her. The maid, whose name was Rosemary, insisted on staying to help her wash her hair. Finally, Kara was left alone to relax in the gorgeous scented hot water which soothed her muscles and tensions. She felt like she had died and gone to heaven. Eventually she got out of her bath and wrapped herself in a large soft fluffy towel. A plate of sweets and chocolates had been placed on the dressing table. Kara picked up a dark chocolate, bit into it and moaned with pleasure. Shaydon was right, it was unlike anything she had ever tasted in her life. She flopped down onto the bed feeling thoroughly pampered.

Rosemary returned carrying a selection of fine dresses. Kara chose a shimmering copper coloured dress. Rosemary highly approved. Once dressed, Rosemary helped her with her hair and applied a light makeup. When Kara finally looked in the mirror, she almost didn't recognise herself. She looked beautiful. The coppery dress fit like a glove and brought out the golden flecks in her brown eyes and hair. She felt amazing.

There was a knock at the door and the maid opened it allowing Shaydon in. His eyes widened at the sight of her.

"Wow, don't you clean up nice. You look stunning Kara."

"You clean up nice too." She smiled back at him before punching him gently on the shoulder. "But you'll always be a scruffy forest ranger to me."

He was dressed in a well fitted crimson shirt and black suit. The crimson worked very well on him, enhancing his confident good looks. His hair had also been washed and he smelled of clean exotic spices.

"Shall we?" He offered Kara his arm which she took laughing.

"Are we even the same people we were about an hour ago?" she asked catching their reflection in a mirror.

"Not bad for a scruffy forest ranger," Shaydon replied, slicking back his hair in mock vanity.

They were shown to the banquet hall which was elaborately decorated for the occasion. Groups of well-dressed people stood around chatting in cliques. Kara noticed there were elegantly laid dining tables to the right of the hall and a band on the left side of the hall playing pleasant music. They were approached by waiters offering exotic canapés and drinks, bursting with rare and unique flavours. Kara found herself running after the waiters for more tastes and samples.

The music changed suddenly… it became more upbeat and Aurora and Melia walked into the hall making a grand entrance. They had also changed into even finer clothes and everyone stared at them appreciating their unique and contrasting beauties. The sisters looked around the room and spotted Kara and Shaydon. Aurora headed towards them while Melia crossed over to the stage and stopped the music to address the crowd.

"Welcome ladies and gentlemen of Arencia. Without further ado let me explain why we have put together this impromptu celebration. We honour the return of Lord Eron's daughter, Lady Kara Gabriel of Eliada, who is joined by our greatly missed hero, Colonel Shaydon of Alfsol."

No one had paid Kara and Shaydon any notice moments before, but now all the people in the hall turned interested eyes on them. Kara heard several murmured comments.

"So, it's true."

"Shaydon has returned with Kara."

"The portal must have opened."

"Where have they been?"

Kara felt exposed and on display, a half-eaten canapé in hand.

"Come now people of Arencia. Give a warm welcome to our returning Hero and Lady." Melia clapped loudly and the banquet hall broke into loud applause.

"You look lovely Kara," Aurora said. "Shaydon, as handsome as I remember."

She invited them to join her at the head table. "I believe that stunning eagle is with you." She pointed across to a corner of the hall where Aegle was perched on a decorative golden branch with another beautiful copper eagle. The two eagles appeared to be deep in conversation.

"Yes," Shaydon replied, "We call her Aegle, she is very dear to me."

"What a beautiful creature she is."

Aurora waited for her chair to be pushed in behind her and then gestured for them to sit.

"Jarita and Aegle certainly seem to have sparked a friendship," she turned to Kara. "Jarita is our copper eagle, the mascot of Arencia. She flies to the other regions and brings news. Only Melia and I are able to understand her in Arencia, and some wise ones from the higher regions, so we tie notes to her leg to convey messages. Melia has a way with languages and is more adept at translating for Jarita than I am, unfortunately we can't understand all animals and we have had difficulty understanding what Aegle has to say… and Jarita seems unwilling to share what Aegle has told her."

"That's amazing," Kara said in awe to Shaydon. "Imagine what we could learn if we could understand animals."

"You can't force them to tell you everything though," Aurora laughed. "Sometimes they can be rather tight beaked."

Kara watched Melia sashay amongst the guests, some of whom were now making their way to the tables. Melia definitely enjoyed being the centre of attention, speaking loudly and laughing hysterically all the while gulping down canapés and champagne.

Several guests made their way over to Kara and Shaydon, introducing themselves and welcoming them with great curiosity. Shaydon knew some of them and fell into easy conversation with old acquaintances. Kara felt overwhelmed and insecure. She was the daughter of the great Lord Eron and people seemed to be scrutinising her, expecting something more from her. Kara had never before had so much attention and felt expectations of her were high but, as she had never really done anything extraordinary in her life, she felt she was a disappointment.

Aurora leaned towards her and said softly. "Don't worry Kara, just be yourself and that is enough, Arencians can be a tad invasive but they mean no harm."

She offered her a glass of bubbling beverage. "Relax and enjoy yourself."

Kara smiled gratefully at Aurora and looked around. The music was lively, the company was entertaining, delicious food and drink were flowing. She decided to take Aurora's advice and relax and enjoy the vibrancy of Arencia and not put any pressure on herself to be anything more than she was. She listened to Melia loudly regale the guests with colourful anecdotes and risqué jokes, noticing that Melia liked to poke fun at her sister Aurora at any opportunity. Aurora, however, did not seem to notice and appeared to be preoccupied with watching Shaydon… thoughtfully.

Later in the evening, Aurora leaned close to Kara again. "I need some fresh air, care to join me?"

Kara followed Aurora out onto a large balcony. There was a handful of people scattered around enjoying the fresh night air. Aurora gestured to an empty bench away from everyone.

"I am worried about Shaydon," she said as she sat down looking around to make sure they weren't overheard. "Underneath the confidence and charisma is a deep grief and I sense guilt shadows him."

"I don't know what you mean," Kara brushed her hair away from her face. "I don't think you need to worry, he's the strongest person I know."

"We knew him as carefree and adventurous before the invasion. His sister Alyne was just the same, a beautiful, brave free spirit. She passed at the uprising and I fear Shaydon feels responsible." Aurora closed her eyes briefly remembering. "You see Shaydon's father, Aldridge discovered Narcissa's decoy and entrusted Shaydon to take his mother and sister to safety in Evergreen, but Shaydon was very young, he was impatient to get back to the battle and had turned a blind eye when Alyne slipped away. She did not want to go into hiding, she was raised amongst warriors and she wanted to fight. Like Shaydon she was anxious to join the battle. Later after the battle had concluded they learned that Alyne had been seen fighting Safiri some distance away. A few soldiers had rushed to her aid but Safiri had disappeared suddenly leaving Alyne for dead amongst the flame lilies where she had fallen."

A cricket chirped on the potted rose bush nearby, startling them both.

"You think Shaydon blames himself?"

"Yes," Aurora looked into Kara's eyes sadly and took her hand, squeezing it gently. "I think you remind him of her."

She looked up at the sky where clouds were covering the stars. "The strange thing is that when they went to retrieve Alyne's body… it had disappeared, there was only a pile of ashes remaining and Alyne's sun locket, which Shaydon now wears in memory of her."

A light drizzle of rain had started to fall, Aurora dabbed at her eyes.

"Aldridge had turned on Shaydon in those moments, blaming him for not ensuring Alyne's safety, his pain and wrath were great. Shaydon swore to avenge Alyne's passing before he left The Realm in search of Safiri. His last memory of his father is extremely painful. Now he has returned with Safiri hot on his heels, unavenged. Only to discover that his beloved mother has lain in a coma all these years. I can imagine he has some reservations about reuniting with his father."

"Does his father still blame him?" Kara asked.

Aurora paused before replying. "I don't know, however, Safiri will come here, and he will come with an army. Shaydon should be encouraged to reunite with his father and make amends as soon as possible. Shaydon was the most promising of young warriors at that time, he had incredible skills and instincts. I requested that he mentor some of our Arencian boys who were training to take up guardian posts because I was so impressed with him. However, he should not try to take on Safiri alone. Together with his father they will surely defeat Safiri, but I have a bad feeling that I cannot shake."

"Why are you so sure that Safiri will come back?"

"Because he needs his awful mother's approval, as well as vengeance in her so-called honour. Not to mention he seeks power and glory as well." Aurora scowled. "But these dangerous times were brought about by his villainous mother. Honourable parents make mistakes from time to time, especially if in a state of bereavement as Aldridge did. But Narcissa was a destructive, self-serving, vile creature. She used her son for her own selfish, controlling purposes without a care or worry for his well-being. Safiri was only a pawn to her. Yes, she would sometimes lavish him with affection, if it suited her, but then she would withdraw that affection in an instant, the moment things didn't go her way, treating him with absolute disdain, cruelty or disregarding him altogether. She created the monster he is today."

The rain came down heavier and lightning flashed in the distance. Aurora and Kara stood up. The few people on the balcony rushed inside.

"Narcissa was a toxic parent to Safiri, but eventually the child becomes the adult and is then responsible for their choices and actions. We all have an inner guidance of what is right for us, sadly some beings ignore their intuitive voices and listen to their egos instead." Aurora took Kara's arm. "Come, we are getting soaked."

They returned to the banquet, spirits and clothes dampened.

"I'm tired, I think I'm going to get out of these wet clothes and go to bed," Kara said quietly to Shaydon.

Shaydon looked up concerned. "Are you ok?"

"Yes I'm fine, I just need to sleep."

Despite Melia's loud protests both Kara and Aurora excused themselves and retired for the night.

Once alone in her room Kara mulled over Aurora's words. She felt deeply sorry for Shaydon and what he had been through. In a strange way she felt sorry for Safiri too. She knew how Dajo's words had affected her own self confidence and independence. *But each of us chooses our own path.* She thought as she lay her head on the plump, soft pillow.

Chapter Five

The Eagle's Warning

Kara could not remember having any dreams when she woke the next morning. She stretched and yawned, enjoying the feel of the soft sheets against her skin. She didn't want to leave the large luxurious bed but saw that her jeans and T-shirt were washed and folded on a chair and grudgingly decided she would have to get up soon. A back-pack that Lukey had lent her and which contained the gifts of armour and sword was placed on a shelf. As she got dressed, she wondered whether she would ever use the sword and chest plate, she hoped they would have time for a duelling lesson.

Shaydon knocked at the door and they set off in search of breakfast. They found Aurora and Melia seated in a small informal dining room. The sisters appeared to be deep in conversation, Melia was somehow more subdued and quieter than the day before. They both smiled warmly as Kara and Shaydon joined them. The breakfast did not disappoint, and they enjoyed another fragrant feast. Kara and Shaydon both sighed and leaned back gratefully in their chairs wiping their mouths once they had eaten their fill.

"That is a beautiful bracelet you wear Kara," Aurora leaned in to take a closer look. "Do you remember it Melia?"

Melia's eyes were hooded and sad. "Yes, I remember it."

She stood up abruptly with the air of someone who had just reached a decision. "Shaydon, Kara there is something I need to talk to you about, will you join me for a walk by the lake?"

Outside the sky was overcast, a dull grey compared to the beautiful azure it had been the day before. The shore was deserted except for a few birds who called out to each other in melancholy tones. Kara felt that a heavy sadness hung in the air. The lake waters were unsettled this morning. They walked on in silence for a while before Melia spoke.

"When I was younger, I used to sneak out of The Realm and visit Faylin quite often. I have always found the earth and its inhabitants very interesting," she smiled wistfully at Kara. "Of course I haven't had a chance to go back there since the portal shut down." She hesitated and bent to pick up a small pebble and examined it closely before flinging it into the lake.

"The last time I was there I went much further than Faylin Forest. I came across a barren place filled with bare rocks. At first, I thought there was no life there but then I found some very strange creatures. They were vile and toad like, but they were also intriguing and entertaining and, in spite of myself, I ended up spending many hours with them. They were very interested in me and professed to being able to see the future, so I took the thick mud like drink they offered and allowed them to read the dregs at the bottom of the cup… they told me everything I wanted to hear and more. They assured me that true love and marriage were my immediate destiny."

She hesitated, the emotions of the memory reflected in her beautiful face. "Before I returned to Faylin they gifted me with what I thought was an ordinary mask. It was ugly and toadish, like them, but they assured me that the mask had magical powers and I should use it with great care."

Then a look of distaste crossed Melia's features. "I soon discovered that I could appear to be anyone I wished to be for a short while, the illusion would only last for thirty minutes or so before the mask would tighten and constrict my breathing and I would be forced to pull it off."

She paused to pick up another pebble and smiled wryly. "I had a lot of fun with that mask but caused a lot of mischief and mayhem too. When Aurora found out about it she was in grave distress, she warned me it was evil and begged me to destroy it, but I wouldn't listen to her."

"Where is the mask now?" Shaydon asked.

"I don't know," Melia answered truthfully. "Shortly after I had received the mask Safiri began visiting me frequently. We became very close. Or at least I thought we were close." She threw the pebble angrily into the water. Thunder stirred in the distance.

Shaydon put his hand reassuringly on Melia's shoulder. "It's okay. You can tell us."

"I found Safiri exciting, passionate, dark and brooding. My senses were overwhelmed, and I mistook my intrigue and passion for feelings of love. I thought I had Safiri wrapped around my little finger, but in truth Safiri had been grooming me. I was under his spell. By the time he told me of his plans to take over The Realm, I was in too deep. My instincts screamed to keep away from him and expose him but I convinced myself that I alone could change him, that all he needed was a stable loving relationship. I would have done anything in my power to make him happy. And he knew this, it was all part of the plan." Angry tears filled her eyes.

Kara reached out to her. "It's going to be alright."

"You don't understand!" Melia pulled away. "All of this is my fault, the invasion, everything. I gave Safiri the mask and Narcissa then had the perfect opportunity to kill Caine, deceive the Alfsol warriors and bring in her dark army... if I hadn't given Safiri the mask none of this would have happened!"

Thunder clapped above them and lightning struck nearby. The lake waters stirred themselves into a frenzy as the heavens suddenly opened and rain slashed down. Shaydon and Kara looked at each other in panic.

"We have to get out of the storm!" Shaydon grabbed Kara and Melia and pulled them away from the shore to the shelter of a large solid tree. They huddled under its branches praying lightning wouldn't strike it.

Shaydon shook Melia gently. "Melia, please, you have to calm down! Take a deep breath... come now, breathe with me." He inhaled and exhaled deeply.

Gradually Melia followed his lead and as she calmed the storm also calmed, until it was just a steady patter of rain. The thunder and lightning stopped. Kara was horrified. Melia's anger had been so intense that she had brought on a superstorm that could have killed them.

Although she had been warned of the temperamental and corporeal energy of Melia, she had not been prepared for this. Usually Kara enjoyed a good rainstorm but this had frightened her.

Melia sat on the ground resting her head on her knees. "Those toad creatures were in cahoots with Narcissa and Safiri, I was the biggest fool and played right into their hands."

She looked up at them teary eyed. "Lives were lost... you were taken from your home... both trapped outside The Realm for years, I am so sorry. I don't expect either of you to forgive me."

Kara and Shaydon looked at each other not knowing what to say.

Eventually Shaydon spoke. "Who else have you told about this Melia?"

"Only Aurora, I have not set foot beyond Arencia ever since. I have been too afraid and ashamed." She sniffed and wiped her nose. "Aurora has been pushing me to tell you the truth since we heard of your arrival."

"Thank you for your honesty," Shaydon spoke softly. "It takes courage to own up to your mistakes, I have made terrible mistakes too." He peered out from under the branches. "See the rain has stopped now. Let's go back to the palace."

During the walk back to the palace the morning started to clear, the sun peeked through the clouds and the spirit of Arencia began to raise again as if a great weight had been removed. The storm had cleared the air and washed away the darkness. Hope and honesty shone through the clouds bringing with it a renewed sense of vitality.

They found Aurora in the throne room. "Did you have a good walk?" She raised a knowing eyebrow. "The weather seems to have been very temperamental this morning." She had just finished reading through some documents when they walked in. She left the papers on the table and went to sit on her throne. Melia followed suit.

"Jarita has gone on the look out for news around The Realm. Aegle has gone with her," Aurora told them.

As if on cue loud screeches wrenched through the air outside. They all looked around in alarm. Jarita and Aegle swept into the throne room beating their wings in agitation. Both sisters leapt up. Jarita landed on Melia's shoulder, pecking impatiently at her.

"Already?" Asked Melia incredulously. "Safiri is here!"

Shaydon swiftly drew his sword. "Where is he?"

"He is at the entrance to Sanguinavia, he is accompanied by a large army. The dwarves and Thendra are standing their ground but Jarita fears the army will break through by day end."

"I'm going to help them!" Shaydon strode to the doors.

"Wait!" called Aurora, running to stop him at the doors. "Wait!" She repeated firmly holding out her hand. "Shaydon, you need to go to your father first. Gather the Alfsol forces, it is the only way to defeat Safiri's army."

Shaydon hesitated.

"Aurora is right. How long will it take us to get to your father?" Asked Kara.

"It won't take long," Aurora said. "Come with me Shaydon we have been looking after someone for you."

They followed her quickly to the palace stables where a handsome large black stallion grazed in a paddock.

"Elash!" Shaydon cried. "My horse!"

"We found Elash wondering our boarders soon after you left, we have taken care of him ever since... with you father's knowledge of course because we could not lure him back to Alfsol. It is as if he has been waiting for you, knowing this time of need would come. He has been kept fit and strong and will get you to Alfsol in no time at all."

Shaydon tearfully embraced Elash for several moments, unable to compose himself. Elash was just as moved by the return of his master. Aurora pulled Kara away from the intimate scene and took her to another stable. There stood a strong chestnut pony.

"Meet Boomer, he is the second fastest horse in our stables. He is well trained and knows the way to Alfsol. He is a good companion to Elash and will be able to keep pace."

"Thank you, Aurora, he is perfect," Kara admired the sleek gelding.

"You must go immediately," Aurora said before calling to the grooms to saddle up the horses.

"What will you do?" Kara asked. "Will you be safe?"

"Melia and I will gather our people in our Safe Fort where they will be out of harm's way. We will send some of our guards to assist in Sanguinavia, some will remain here to keep fort."

The horses were saddled within a few minutes and Kara and Shaydon quickly mounted, adrenaline coursing through their veins.

"God speed!" Aurora called behind Kara and Shaydon as they cantered out of the stables."

Chapter Six

Alfsol

T he sun was blazing high in the sky as they galloped through the countryside. They had been riding uphill for some time but the horses were strong and eager and did not slow down. Alfsol was situated on higher grounds. Kara could hear drums beating in the distance ahead.

"The drums of war!" Shaydon called back to her. "Alfsol is preparing for battle!"

The ground levelled out briefly as they passed through a small meadow of poppy flowers and then ascended steeply again, the hill was covered in giant sunflowers. The horses slowed to a trot, frothing with sweat and excitement. A warm glow emanated from Shaydon that Kara had never seen before, she watched him in awe, becoming aware of a warm light resonating in her own solar plexus. They soon came upon the drums which were found in a large clearing at the top of the hill. Thousands of formidable looking warriors were preparing for battle. There were cannons being made ready, swords and axes being sharpened, bows being strung. War horses were stomping on the ground, neighing impatiently. Both Elash and Boomer loudly announced their arrival, braying over the other horses. All the warriors wore similar golden armour to Kara and Shaydon's. A dozen men marched towards them, one of whom blew a horn calling the attention of all of the other warriors. Shaydon dismounted Elash and put his hands up in the air calling a peaceful greeting to the warriors.

The soldier with the horn announced. "Behold the return of Colonel Shaydon!"

After a moment's silence the field of warriors erupted into explosive applause. Kara watched as Shaydon became overwhelmed with emotion, tears poured down his cheeks as he disappeared under the embrace of several warriors. Kara leaned forward stroking Boomer's neck trying to keep him calm as he pranced nervously. Several minutes passed before Shaydon appeared at her side and helped her to dismount.

"Let's go and meet my father." He wiped at his eyes. They handed the horses to one of the soldiers and followed the dozen men to the back of the clearing where there was a row of yellow pavilions. The yellow and green striped main pavilion stood in the centre.

"We've been expecting you Shaydon," said an extremely tall warrior. "Our scouts saw you coming, time has not changed you much and so you were recognised at once." He turned to Kara. "Rumour has it that my lady is none other than Kara Gabriel?"

"Yes, this is Kara Gabriel, daughter of Lord Eron." Shaydon replied. The soldiers stopped in their tracks and started to remove their helmets and kneel before her.

Kara looked around anxiously, she did not want to cause any distraction to the rest of the warriors and would have preferred to remain unknown.

"Your return inspires our great warriors." The tall man spoke again. "Although our Alfsol men are undefeated in their courage and bravery your presence only strengthens their convictions. Our victory is assured in this battle." He turned to the soldiers. "Rise good men. Go and confirm our Lady Kara's return. Protect our Realm fiercely. The time has come to prove Alfsol's might, worth and honour."

The warriors dispersed to spread the word of Kara's return. Only the tall warrior stayed to accompany them.

"Commander Aldridge awaits you inside." He placed his hand on Shaydon's shoulder looking down gently as they paused before the main pavilion. "This is the first time I have seen him happy since…" he broke off and pulled the curtain aside.

Inside the pavilion was a large table with a group of war councillors gathered around it, deep in discussion. At the centre stood a tall, strong and stern weathered man. His fair hair and trimmed beard showed flecks of grey. He had the same chiseled cheeks and jawbone as Shaydon. His eyes, however, were a startling deep blue. They seemed familiar to Kara, but she could not think why. He looked up as the warrior announced their arrival. Both Shaydon and Aldridge stood, frozen, for several moments before they rushed at each other meeting in a gruff and emotional embrace. They held each other for several more moments before letting go and looking each other squarely in the eyes.

"Welcome home, my son," Aldridge finally found his voice. "Your absence has worn heavily upon me."

Two older ladies broke from the council and ran to Shaydon, embracing him and wiping the tears from their eyes. Shaydon grinned widely hugging them both tightly to him. Although the women were older, they were strong, fit and dressed for battle. They looked like fearless warriors and Kara thought they resembled lionesses.

"Kara, meet my aunts Kit and Len," Shaydon introduced them. They had the same jewel like blue eyes as their brother Aldridge.

"Are you really Kara Gabriel?" Kit asked.

"But you were just a teeny tiny babe?" Len looked at her in wonder.

"Yes-" Kara was engulfed in a bear like hug. The two aunts almost squeezed the breath out of her.

"Oh, so much to celebrate!" Kit cried happily. "Both Shaydon and Kara! I wondered whether I would ever see this day."

"Unfortunately, there is a battle to tend to before we start celebrating," Len and Kit released Kara.

"Kara it is my greatest pleasure to introduce you to my father, Commander Aldridge," Shaydon's voice was thick with emotion.

Commander Aldridge bowed low to Kara. "An honour," he said in his deep soothing voice which was so much like Shaydon's.

Kara noticed that he had a large emerald gem embedded in the centre of his armour as opposed to the citrine stone which adorned the armour of Shaydon, Kit and Len.

"Shaydon my son, there is so much to say. Perhaps we will be blessed with a few private moments. My heart is fit to burst at the sight of you." He placed his hand on his chest, "But war is upon us and there is no time now. I am proud to have you fight by my side once more. We have sent word to Sanguinavia to stand back and let Safiri's army pass through. Thendra and dwarves are to follow the enemy at a safe distance. We will descend upon Safiri with all our force while thendra, dwarves and guards of Arencia will block his retreat. I am encouraged to hear that Xylia is accompanying our brave folk from the lower regions."

"I have waited a long time for this," Shaydon's lips tightened and fists clenched.

"Safiri travels with a wagon of toad-like creatures. Together they command a large army of assorted shadow beings. The most powerful are the Dark Ones who spread doom by exuding fear and doubt into the hearts of those who try to stand in their way." Len told them, a deep frown burrowing her brow.

"They strike terror and weaken the will of those who face them," Kit said darkly. "There are also a number of zombie creatures, recently risen from graves by the looks of them, but we are not too concerned about them."

"It is the Dark Ones we must overcome; they do not fight physically, they fight the will and aim to steal the soul," Aldridge stated. "But I have every confidence in the light-force of Alfsol." He grinned at Shaydon. "We also have Drakontus who is ready to make his debut."

Shaydon's eyes widened. "The dragon is alive? But is he ready? What practice has he had?"

"He has been taken on some runs, he is young but he should have enough fire in him for one fly around."

Kara could feel the excitement bouncing off father and son. "You have a dragon?" She asked incredulously.

"Drakontus was newly hatched at the time of Narcissa's invasion, but his mother Drakina was old and passed away before he was born, I assumed he could not have survived without her," Shaydon explained.

"We no longer think that Drakina passed from old age as she was only two hundred years old, you will remember her mate, father of Drakontus, lived to be two hundred and seventy or so. After the invasion, Lord Eron managed to communicate with dragon experts from the higher dimensions. They suggested that Drakina had been poisoned, we suspect Narcissa and Safiri of course." Aldridge stroked his chin, "our warriors could not let the last dragon of The Realm die. They worked tirelessly to nurture and raise him. He is extremely strong, though still young and inexperienced.... today we are eager to see how he handles battle."

"Safiri will have some idea of our strategy," said Shaydon. "Let's hope he has no idea of Drakontus's survival."

"Every precaution has been taken to hide our secret weapon, not many outside of Alfsol know that our dragon lives," Aldridge proudly folded his arms. "We are ready for Safiri's army."

"Are the people of Arencia and Sanguinavia safe?" Kara asked.

"The way to Alfsol is purposefully open to Safiri, drawing him away from the lower regions. Each region has a safe hold to protect its people. We counted on Safiri not wanting to waste time there. His sights are set here and beyond, we are informed he has passed through both regions with minimal damage."

Aldridge straightened his back and turned to instruct his sisters. "Kit and Len, we must ensure Kara's safety. Please take her to our fortress and guard her well."

Kara wanted to stay and started to protest.

"You must go Kara," Shaydon insisted before she could object. "I know you want to stay and fight but you aren't ready yet. You'll be safe with my aunts and I need to focus all my attention on this battle."

"But-" Kara started.

"Go Kara, I could never forgive myself if something happened to you."

Kara thought of Shaydon's mother and Alyne before she reluctantly agreed. She hugged him impulsively, biting back tears. "Be safe," she whispered.

Boomer, with Kit's and Len's horses waited for her outside the pavilion. They mounted and rode beyond the clearing into pleasant gardens. Flame lilies sprung in abundance from the ground and Kara wondered if this was where Alyne had lain. They complained about the intensely hot weather and were grateful to find some respite under the cool shade of a clump of large trees. Kara wondered why Aldridge had an emerald embedded in his armour and not a citrine stone.

"He wears the emerald in honour of his beloved wife Katran, Shaydon's mother." Kit ducked under low hanging branches, then continued. "Katran is from the Evergreen region, where she lies now. She was not an Alfsol warrior and never understood war."

"Shaydon looks so much like her," Len smiled sadly. "They were a very close family."

"Katran was stricken down with grief at the loss of Alyne and the disappearance of Shaydon. She has lain in a deep coma these past years," Kit continued. "Aldridge refuses to give up hope, he insists she will wake one day, but I fear it has been too long."

Kara considered the loss and grief Shaydon and his father had suffered because of Safiri and Narcissa, she wondered how many more families had been affected by them. The thought of Shaydon's mother lying in a coma led her to wonder about her own biological mother....*why had no one ever spoken of her in The Realm*? She also remembered Maja with love and was glad that she was safe in her cottage far away in another world.

A massive golden fortress loomed ahead of them as they rode the rest of the way in silence. A large moat surrounded the fortress and a drawbridge was let down allowing them to enter. Inside the fortress were several more soldiers and strong looking women and children. They all had fierce and determined looks on their faces and demanded news from Kit and Len. Their expressions changed to wonder, hope then joy when Kara was introduced and a golden aura slowly filled the fortress, beaming outwards from the people.

"The winds of change have begun."

"Welcome Lady Kara, past wrongs will be righted."

"The worst is surely over."

The people gathered around them; their faces glowed in renewed confidence.

"You see the light and strength of the Alfsol people. It is our inner light which we are taught to use for protection and power." Kit explained the golden glow emanating from the people as they excused themselves and headed for a staircase. "Our inner light projects outwards as the courage within us grows."

"Shaydon tried to teach me about this light-force, but I didn't really understand it… until now, I can actually see it here in the people." Kara looked around in awe as they reached the stairs. "When I spoke to him of my nightmares about Safiri, he encouraged me to imagine I had this light within me and to envision it growing and protecting me."

"Every being has this spark within them, but not everyone knows it," said Kit, "here in Alfsol, we are taught to use it from the day we are born."

"You'll soon see the intensity of its power." Len led the way. "We can watch from the high towers."

Kara followed Kit and Len up hundreds of stairs. They climbed for a long time and Kara was quite out of breath when they finally reached the top. They clambered out onto a large flat roof bordered by a parapet.

Telescopes were strategically placed along the parapet. Kara adjusted one of the telescopes to look upon the Alfsol warriors below. They were lined up and ready for battle.

The cannons were set in front, the archers behind the cannons. Many rows of warriors with swords drawn sat on horseback behind the archers. It was an impressive sight. Shaydon, mounted on Elash, faced the army while his father rode up and down the frontline, holding his sword high, shouting words of encouragement, rousing his warriors for battle.

Much further down the hill appeared a massive swarm gaining momentum. Kara adjusted her telescope to get a better look. She gasped as she spied Safiri. He was just as she remembered him from her nightmares. Dark skinned with blazing coals for eyes. He rode an evil looking black horse which appeared to have the same demon eyes as his master. Riding next to Safiri was a carriage of vile toad like creatures, their skin a slimy translucent green. The fat bulging female in front of the carriage had a long-forked tongue which swished close to Safiri's ear as she spoke to him. She had a purplish red mohican of thick wiry hair sprouting out of her head. Her greedy, sly eyes bulged at the front of her grotesque face. Kara shuddered with repulsion. She sensed this was a very wicked creature.

Dark shadows throughout the evil army caught Kara's attention. They were tall black eerie shapes without faces nor eyes. Kara was filled with a sense of deep despair as she focused on them. Her body filled with dread and she just wanted to lie down on the ground and give up. She pulled the telescope away with effort and spied other various strange zombie like creatures on foot amongst Safiri's army.

She heard Kit and Len say a prayer as the dark army swarmed up the hill towards the Alfsol warriors. The cannons were fired and the shots boomed and echoed for several minutes as the cannon balls blew holes into the dark enemy but the darkness of the shadow beings spread up the hill like a plague of ants. The Alfsol archers released their arrows with force and several of the zombie creatures fell… and then something amazing took place. An enormous golden dragon swooped down on the dark army expelling flames into the mass, the dragon circled twice breathing fire and incinerating almost a quarter of the evil army and knocking out another quarter with its large powerful wings, but the dragon soon weakened and struggled to draw another breath. It flew away haphazardly to the loud applause of the Alfsol warriors. The Alfsol cavalry took advantage of the destruction Drakontus had left in its wake and charged at full speed down the hill to meet the remaining enemy head on.

Kara watched in awe as the warriors lit up and a golden glow beamed down onto the darkness below. The light seemed to momentarily extinguish the darkness but the Dark Ones kept rising. The battle became a huddled mass of dark and light. Kara could see swords and axes flying. Both good and bad falling. Sparks of fire erupting. Some people and creatures scattering. She looked fervently for Shaydon. She could not find him, nor could she see Safiri.

"Safiri has disappeared!" She exclaimed in alarm.

Kit and Len looked through their telescopes urgently.

"He's gone!" Len yelled. "And so have the toads!"

"Let's get Kara to the keep!" Kit ran towards the stairs, sword drawn.

Kara and Len followed, drawing their swords. Kara stumbled and almost fell down the stairs in her haste but Len caught her arm. They could hear screams coming from below as they reached one of the landings. There they spied four of the toads. Kit and Len stood in front of Kara and the strong Alfsol light erupted from the two women with a force of power and strength. The toads rushed at them, forked tongues lashing from their bellowing mouths while they brandished short stout axes and daggers.

Kara instinctively turned around and behind her standing further up on the stairs was a fifth ugly toad, sneering. "Lookey lookey what do we have here? Don't care what master sezz, nasty girlzz are better off dead."

The toad descended the stairs slowly, axe raised and ready to bury in Kara's head. Kara instinctively struck her sword upwards as the toad leapt towards her, thrusting straight into the creature's mid-section. A look of surprise crossed the toad's face before its axe clattered to the ground and the creature dropped to the floor, forked tongue hanging out of its wide mouth. It then dissolved into a pile of dirt which evaporated slowly into thin air.

Suddenly a terrible screech pierced the air next to Kara and she turned quickly, recognising the vile toad who had had its tongue in Safiri's ear earlier. The creature lunged towards her, talons outstretched, aiming to claw out her throat. Kara swung her sword round cleanly slicing off the toad's head. She stumbled backwards, reeling from the force as the head rolled across the floor.

Len ran over to Kara helping her up. "Are you alright?"

"Yes" Kara wobbled slightly as she tried to stand.

"That was incredible Kara!" Len helped to steady her. "You have the natural instincts of a warrior."

They looked around as the dirt remains of the toad creatures evaporated. "I think we got all of them." Kit wiped the sweat from her brow. "All monsters' bodies turn to dust and the remains are sent to a hellish place where they will be trapped for centuries, they won't bother us again."

"How did we miss that one hiding on the stairwell?" Len mused. "The one that attacked Kara from behind."

"Do you think they can teleport?" Kara asked.

"That would explain how they disappeared from the battle so quickly" Kit shook her head. "But this fort is protected from such magic, I have no idea how they got in."

The landing darkened.

"Where is Safiri?" Kara's blood ran cold. Turning slowly, she saw him walking up the opposite stairs.

Kit and Len immediately rushed at him with swords raised, but he knocked them aside with one sweep of his arm. He was expanding with every step he took. He laughed cruelly. Kara heard the sisters' frantic cries, but their warnings were drowned out by the blood pounding in her ears as she raised her sword and charged at Safiri. He burst into flames as his fist slammed into her ribs, her mouth filled with a surge of coppery blood as she bit her tongue, she collapsed to the ground gasping for air and slowly passed out as Safiri towered over her.

She awoke choking and swallowing smoke. Her insides burned in agony, she was doubled over something jostling her innards. She realised that she had been flung over Safiri's shoulder and they were outside in the open air. Panic struck and she began to struggle just before a bright green light filled the surrounding area and a beautiful sound came to her ears. She stopped kicking and tried to look up.

A shimmering white unicorn galloped towards them. There was a very old, but strong, man riding the unicorn, his long beard and hair flowing, he carried a large staff. The green light was beaming from within him and the staff. Kara became aware of a golden eagle flying above the man before she dropped heavily to the ground, her head struck something sharp and the sweet relief of pain-free darkness enfolded her once again.

Chapter Seven

Evergreen

Kara kept her eyes closed not wishing to wake from her safe, calm and reassuring dream. The air around her was light and easy, she breathed deeply. Her spirit was soothed as she walked in the lush greenery past large old weeping willows, a softness under foot. She heard tender voices and bird song in the distance.

Reluctantly she opened one eye to soft pink surroundings. She opened the other eye and slowly looked around. She was lying on a soft comfortable bed in a pale pink room. A window looked out onto a lush green garden similar to that of her dream. There was a vase of fragrant pink roses on the bedside table next to her along with a jug of iced water and a glass. The voices she heard came from the end of her bed. She gingerly raised herself up on her elbows.

Shaydon and an old man were talking, they both turned to smile warmly at her. Shaydon came to her side and kissed her forehead before taking her hand in both of his. He appeared very happy and relaxed.

"Finally you wake," he said squeezing her hand. "How do you feel?"

"Surprisingly good," she rolled her shoulders and stretched her neck. "Where am I?"

"You are in Evergreen," Shaydon said.

The old man approached Kara's other side. "Delighted to meet you Kara," he smiled, pouring her a glass of the iced water. His face was wizened with deep lines and his beautiful soft green eyes looked intensely within her, touching her heart and she felt an uplifting sense of love wind its way around her rough inner edges, melting away any remaining traces of anxiety and discomfort.

"Kara meet The Sage, Custodian of Evergreen," Shaydon released her hand. "The most gifted healer in our Realm and beyond."

"I remember!" Kara gasped. "It was you...you were riding the unicorn...you saved me...I think."

"Indeed," The Sage bowed his head, green eyes twinkling. "I believe we are indebted to you for dispersing of a couple of Themians "

"The toads," Shaydon clarified. "Properly known as Themians. You killed the leader." He said with admiration.

"I did? The leader?" And then she remembered. "Kit? Len? Safiri?!"

"A bit battered and bruised...but they are strong women, they're fine." Shaydon assured her.

"What happened on the battlefield?" Kara leaned back relieved and sipped her water.

"Well Drakontus was spectacular, he obliterated at least half of Safiri's army. Our warriors easily defeated the zombies but we struggled with the Dark Ones....until help came from The Sage." Shaydon looked at the old man with deep gratitude. "Those dark faceless creatures were like none I have ever fought before. Their darkness creeps into you, filling you with hopeless despair, eating at your soul and will."

Kara remembered how lifeless she had felt when she had merely looked at them through a distant telescope. She shuddered imagining how much worse it would be up close while fighting them.

"The light force of Alfsol is powerful, you would have defeated the Dark Ones eventually." The Sage's eyes crinkled. "But when the eagles brought news of Dark Ones within The Realm, I set off for Alfsol immediately."

"Thank the heavens." Shaydon shook his head, still in disbelief. "You diminished the Dark Ones within minutes."

"Ahh the power of love...love conquers all." The Sage chuckled. "I often wonder why the truth is called a cliché on earth."

"It was a sight I'll never forget," Shaydon's eyes lit up as he recounted the scene to Kara. "The Sage rode onto the battlefield his staff beaming a powerful green light, and the Dark Ones just disintegrated before our eyes. The field filled with green and white light and a peaceful sound filled the air."

"That green and white light was the last thing I remember seeing before I passed out," Kara turned to The Sage. "Why is it so powerful?"

"Because it contains pure love." The Sage answered. "Love in its highest form is the antidote to negative vibrations, such as fear and doubt, which is why the Dark Ones were powerless in its presence. Pure love is the greatest power in our lives."

"Oh," Kara frowned, not sure whether she understood completely. "Is it similar to the light-force of Alfsol?"

"The light of Alfsol is a force for personal rule and strength. Every being has this force within them but in Alfsol we are trained to enhance our personal power." Shaydon explained.

"Whereas..." The Sage chimed in, "the light of pure love has no restrictions or ulterior motives, there is no judgement in its force. No attachment either, which makes it the most powerful force. You'll grow to understand it in time and differentiate it from the other light forces."

"I have recently discovered that pure love has the power to heal almost every wound or disease," Shaydon smiled.

"Possibly the only challenge to pure love...is grief." The Sage folded his hands serenely on his chest.

"You'll find that most people from Evergreen have pure open hearts, Evergreen is known for its refreshing healing energy," Shaydon looked out the window wistfully searching for something or someone.

"What happened to Safiri?" Kara sat up again.

"He escaped along with a few Themians," Shaydon turned back from the window frowning.

"He escaped!" Kara was upset. "What does that mean for us...and The Realm?"

"He will return," The Sage answered. "The wish of his mother lies strong within him, Safiri hides and waits. Lord Eron, your father, is the only person who has the ability to free her. Safiri will not kill you Kara. He wishes to bargain your life in some way, it is part of his plan. He is not far away."

Kara looked in alarm at Shaydon who nodded gravely.

"Do not be alarmed Kara. I assure you are very safe here in Evergreen. This is the most protected region within The Realm." The Sage leaned forward to plump up her pillows. "No harm will come to you here."

"Can't we just stay here forever then?" Asked Kara, feeling despondent already knowing the answer.

"Your journey does not end here Kara Gabriel. But you do not have to think of leaving straight away, at least until I am confident that you have healed completely, which will be soon, you are very strong." The Sage stepped back. "You must be hungry; you have been unconscious for three days."

Kara's stomach grumbled loudly in reply and The Sage chuckled again before excusing himself to organise a meal for her.

"Kara, I've so much to tell you," Shaydon grinned, his joy was infectious. "Wonderful news!"

"Don't make me wait then...tell me," Kara laughed.

There was a knock at the door and a beautiful young woman entered the room. Her golden hair tumbled down her shoulders and back, her sapphire blue eyes lit up when she saw Kara sitting up in bed. She ran to Kara's side embracing her tightly.

"Oh Kara!" She exclaimed. "I'm so glad to see you awake and well."

Kara looked at Shaydon in confusion. His brown eyes gleamed with moisture. "Kara, this is my sister, Alyne."

"What?!" Kara nearly fell out of bed.

Alyne laughed and her blue eyes twinkled mischievously. "It's true. I'm Alyne...but you may know me better as Aegle."

"This doesn't make any sense..." Kara looked from brother to sister. "You are...were Aegle?"

"I was Aegle," Alyne confirmed.

Kara stared at Alyne is disbelief and then squinted. "Your eyes... your eyes are the same as Aegle's."

"Yes, I have my father's eyes."

"But how?"

"We'll explain, but first you must eat, you need to regain your strength." Shaydon interrupted as a healer came in with a tray of food.

Kara stared at the assortment of toast, honey and strawberries. She was torn between ravenous hunger and burning desire to find out what had happened.

Alyne poured her a cup of herbal tea and then buttered a piece of toast. "Once you've eaten something I'll tell you everything... dig in!" Alyne handed her the toast.

Kara was so hungry that she gulped down her meal in mere minutes. The Sage returned as she sipped her tea and they all sat around her bed in happy camaraderie.

"We have become aware that Safiri has the ability of teleportation. Very few beings in our Realm possess this ability," said The Sage. "Apparently this is something he has in common with the Themians."

"When the invasion took place all those years ago, I snuck onto the outskirts of the battle and came face to face with Safiri," Alyne took Shaydon's hand. "He knocked me out cold and teleported with me to earth. He then immediately teleported back to Alfsol and used that infamous mask to impersonate me lying still on the ground so the warriors would report I was dead. Meanwhile in reality, I woke to find myself alone and unguarded on earth. I'm not sure what he wanted to do with me."

"Prisoners of war are used for bargaining purposes," said The Sage. "Safiri obviously took possession of the mask from his mother before she was captured."

"Melia confessed to Kara and I that she was the one who brought the mask into The Realm. She was tricked into it by the Themians and then conned into giving it to Safiri," said Shaydon "Which is how the invasion began, with Narcissa poisoning her husband before impersonating him."

"Safiri soon realised that Narcissa was going to lose the battle," said The Sage, "so he attempted to collect as much collateral as he could...but his plans went awry. He kidnapped you from Eliada while your father was involved in the battle, Kara. We suspect Safiri must have used the mask to disguise himself as one of your nursemaids." The Sage leaned back in his chair. "Luckily word was sent in time to Xylia of Faylin Forest and she stopped Safiri from making away with you."

"But what happened to you Alyne?" Kara asked.

"I had been left in a barren place of giant sharp rocks, not a blade of grass nor a tree to be seen anywhere," shuddered Alyne. "I clambered over the rocks, praying for help, trying to find a way out of there. I was so afraid and had no idea where I was."

She paused to look out the window at the lush Evergreen garden before continuing. "I was weak and injured, full of scratches and grazes from scrambling over the rocks, and then, my prayers were answered. A Guardian of the Earth found me; her name was Abellona. She had an affinity with the Sun and fire. She cared for me but she couldn't stay with me, as is the rule of earth guardians, after a short while we agreed that in order to keep me safe she should transform me into an eagle so I could fly free to find my way home."

"I had no idea Aegle was my sister when she found me," Shaydon said regretfully.

"How could you know?" Alyne smiled at him before turning back to Kara. "Once we had returned to The Realm I was eager to fly to Evergreen... to The Sage, I knew he would know who I was and have the power to transform me back to my real self."

"Both Aegle and Jarita swept into my garden calling me to Alfsol's aid," said The Sage. "Mystique had also found his way back to me the day before and so we rode like the wind into the battle."

"Mystique?" Kara raised an eyebrow. "The unicorn from Faylin Forest?"

"Yes, the one and only," replied The Sage. "It is Mystique who alerted Xylia that Safiri had kidnapped you all those years ago. A brave and honourable creature. In saving you he, himself became trapped in Faylin Forest."

"I'm so sorry that happened to him."

"Don't be sorry my dear." The Sage patted her hand. "I knew Mystique would be safe with Xylia in Faylin, one cannot usually hold a unicorn in one place for too long, because they are free spirits but Faylin is a unique and special forest and he was very comfortable there. Needless to say, I am very happy he is back in Evergreen for now. I missed him terribly. He actually came back with the news of your and Shaydon's return."

"You can communicate with animals then?" Kara asked.

"Yes, I am honoured to be able to do so. There are a few of us. Xylia, Aurora and Melia, no doubt Alyne will also be able to now." The Sage winked at Alyne.

"Strangely enough when I tried to communicate with Xylia on earth, and later with Aurora and Melia in Arencia, they couldn't understand me as Aegle." Alyne shook her head. "I was able to communicate with birds perfectly though, but not with other creatures. It has been a strange, sometimes frustrating journey for me. I connected with Jarita immediately of course, because she is an eagle, also a very wise being. She advised me not to disclose who I was until we reached Evergreen, she thought it would be too much of a distraction for my father and Shaydon so close to battle."

Shaydon put his arm around his sister's shoulders. "I sometimes have to pinch myself to make sure I'm not dreaming and that you're really here."

He turned to face Kara. "After the battle, The Sage insisted my father and I follow him back to Evergreen. We were reluctant to leave Alfsol straight after the battle but I'm so glad we did. I also wanted to ensure you were alright Kara." Tears filled his eyes. "And when we arrived here The Sage transformed Aegle back to Alyne before our eyes.... We hadn't suspected anything, it was miraculous, the colours, the light-force, the sound, it was the most beautiful and powerful transformation. My father and I were brought to our knees."

Kara was struck by the revelation and tears rolled down her cheek. Alyne dabbed at her eyes too.

The Sage stood up. "Divine timing," he said. "It all worked out as it was supposed to. Now Kara," he gently took her arm, "do you feel ready to stand, maybe get a little exercise? You took quite a blow from Safiri... but the Evergreen gardens are healing grounds, good for your mind, body and spirit, a walkabout will do wonders for you." He helped her into a standing position.

"Is she up to more news?" Shaydon asked The Sage.

"Of course," The Sage handed Alyne a soft pink dressing gown and slippers which she helped Kara into.

"Good!" Alyne beamed. "I can't wait for you to meet our mother."

Kara froze in shock. "Your mother?" She glanced at Shaydon who looked fit to burst with happiness.

"Yes," he grinned unabashedly. "I told you I had lots of wonderful news."

Kara, Shaydon and Alyne strolled through the graceful, soothing gardens of Evergreen. The green grass was as soft as she remembered from her dreams, charming weeping willows rested by clear ponds of water. The sky was a soft pink. Evergreen reminded Kara of Arencia, but the atmosphere in Evergreen was consistently healing and spiritual. In Arencia the weather was temperamental and ever changing.

As they walked Shaydon and Alyne spoke of their mother's recovery. The Sage had told them how he had never lost hope of her return to health because every time their father Aldridge would visit her, Katran's eyes would flutter, her breathing would quicken and her cheeks would flush. She would react the same way whenever her children were mentioned. The Sage realised that Katran had no desire to wake due to the grief she felt at losing her children and only their return would break through this deep depressing sleep.

Shaydon, Alyne and Aldridge went to her soon after Alyne's transformation. They spoke together by her side for several long minutes, laying their hands gently upon her and little by little she regained consciousness, eventually waking from her long dark night of the soul. The spirit of Evergreen had miraculously kept her alive until her family was brought back to her, whole and intact.

"The Sage is right; the power of love is the greatest power there is." Alyne parted some weeping branches for them to pass through.

They entered a small private garden nook which was filled with pink rose blossoms. There was a couple seated on a love bench. Kara recognised Commander Aldridge. The woman was lovely and serene, she had long dark hair and gentle brown eyes. Kara could immediately see she was Shaydon's mother, he definitely took his looks from his mother as Alyne took hers from her father. Katran rose to greet them and her children went straight to her open arms.

Kara bit back emotional tears while Shaydon introduced her to his mother.

Katran embraced Kara gently. "Thank you for bringing my children safely home."

"They brought me safely home," Kara smiled.

"My heart sings, finally free from pain. All of you are back where you belong," Katran sighed.

Being in the presence of such a loving mother, Kara felt her own heart open a little wider.

They all walked through the gardens, talking of earth and the lost years whilst enjoying each moment of being together. Aldridge looked years younger than he had appeared when Kara had met him, just days before.

Eventually Shaydon turned sombrely to his mother "I've dreamed of this reunion every day these past years and I treasure every second of it, but you know I must leave soon. I wish to accompany Kara through the higher regions to Eliada."

"I know, my son," Katran stroked his cheek. "I wish I could keep you all here with me...but we cannot deprive Lord Eron of his daughter for much longer," she took her husband's arm. "We understand this better than anyone."

"I wish I could understand," Kara brushed her hair out of her eyes. "Why can't my father come here and meet me in Evergreen?"

Katran smiled sadly. "Here in The Realm we believe that the journey is just as important as the destination. You must reach your destination, Kara. Of course, it is your choice if you decide to stop at a certain place and stay there, but that would be a shame. You were taken from your home and now you need to find your way back there. Your father waits for you, I imagine his impatience, but he knows that he must not interfere with your journey. You still have lessons to learn. You will understand our ways in time, I hope."

"There is also Safiri to contend with," Shaydon said tensely, rubbing his neck. "He lays low and waits within The Realm. Waiting for the right moment to strike. We need to make him pay for all the years he has stolen from us."

"You must try to understand Safiri," Katran said gently touching Shaydon's arm. "If you can understand your enemy you will have an advantage. He did not have the mother's love he deserved to have. Fate dealt him a cruel blow with the circumstances he was born into."

"We are all born with free will," Aldridge stated. "Safiri's father was a good man, Safiri could have chosen to follow his father's path but he chose the evil ways of his mother."

"Commander Caine was under Narcissa's power, he was blind to her cruel treatment of their son, and so he did nothing to protect Safiri," Katran protested. "I used to feel so sorry for that little boy."

"Can you tell me about Narcissa?" Kara asked.

"Narcissa truly believed that she was superior to everyone. It is a mystery to me where she came from. Some believed she was from a quiet, unknown part of

Alfsol. Others thought her temperament was likened to those of Arencia," Katran replied. "I always had my doubts about her, but Commander Caine was so in love with her that we respected his choice... and at first we were happy for him. However, it soon became clear to me that Narcissa was very ambitious and considered the people of the Rainbow Realm to be beneath her. Such elitism isolates the heart, she openly scorned her husband's compassion and loyalty to The Realm and she felt burdened by her son's need for her care and attention."

"It was Katran's concerns that made me doubt the decoy on that fateful day." Aldridge looked at his wife with a mixture of love and regret.

They walked on in silence for a while, letting the surroundings comfort them, until Katran spoke again. "Being in the presence of a person with a powerfully closed heart throws everyone around them into some form of doubt, even I was affected when I was in Narcissa's company. Imagine being consistently exposed to that. Closed hearts are so damaging, try to find some compassion for Safiri, We cannot regain the years we have lost but we can appreciate every moment we have now, whilst honouring the lessons we have learnt."

"And what of Safiri's lessons?" Shaydon said through tight lips. "He is a tyrant who runs free."

"Yes," Katran agreed. "But I don't want bitterness to ruin any of your lives. Forgiveness is not giving up on justice that needs to be served, nor does it remove or alter the pain and sorrow of the years we lost, but forgiveness can make our present and future days less painful. Safiri did wrong and we cannot excuse his behavior, and he will surely suffer the consequences of it."

She paused to smell a rose. "I know there is a time and place for forgiveness. It cannot be forced, but when you are ready to forgive, you do so for yourself, for your own freedom and happiness."

Shaydon shook his head. "I don't know if I'll ever be ready to forgive him."

"I know you have good intentions Mama." Alyne put her arm around Katran, "but for now we still feel raw about the years that were lost to us, in time, perhaps, we'll be able to forgive."

"I can't help but feel a bit sorry for Safiri," Kara said. "I have met him so many times in my dreams... nightmares. The more I hear about his relationship with his mother the more I think his acts are all for her love and approval, it seems he can't see her for the monster she is."

"You are wise beyond your years Kara," Katran took her hand. "A credit to your father."

They continued to walk through the peaceful surroundings, no one mentioned Safiri again. Some way ahead of them they saw a beautiful girl sitting on a bench by a small pond. She was engrossed in a book. Shaydon stopped abruptly, squaring his shoulders and straightening his clothes. Katran and Alyne raised knowing eyebrows at each other while Aldridge tried to hide a smile.

"That's Tealia," Alyne whispered to Kara. "The Sage's daughter."

Tealia looked up just then and smiled. She got up to approach them. She had long black hair and turquoise eyes the same colour as the pond she had been sitting beside.

She greeted them all warmly and smiled shyly at Shaydon before looking to Kara.

"Kara I am glad to see you are awake now. You look very well." She held out her hand to Kara. "I am Tealia. I have heard so much about you, it is my pleasure."

Kara was wondering why she hadn't heard of Tealia before now as it was quite evident that   Shaydon was completely smitten by her, but she smiled and shook Tealia's hand.

෴

The next couple of days were spent resting, regrouping and centring themselves. Although Kara enjoyed getting to know Shaydon's family it made her long to meet with her own kin. Spending time with Katran evoked memories of Maja. Kara had never felt deprived of a mother as Maja had been such a loving foster parent despite her shortcomings. She missed Maja and was comforted in the knowledge that Maja was safe back in the cottage at the edge of Faylin Forest. The days spent in Evergreen had Kara frequently wondering about her real mother. *Who was she and why was there barely any mention of her here in Rainbow Realm?* Whenever she asked about her, she was told that her mother was a very special woman but her story would be best explained by her father, Lord Eron.

"Your mother was somewhat of a mystery to us here in The Realm," Katran said. "Because we know so little about her we cannot tell you much. I do know that she was very special, good and kind. She was the love of your father's life."

"Why do you speak in past tense?" Kara had urged. "What happened to her?"

"I wouldn't want to tell you anything of which I am not certain," Katran squeezed Kara's hand. "It is best to leave this tale to your father who will know the whole truth of it."

A bond was forming between Kara, Alyne and Tealia, although Alyne and Tealia were somewhat older than Kara, they reminded her in small ways of her good friends Lina and Tawny back home. Kara and Tealia shared a love of books and spent many hours in Tealia's library discussing and comparing the different books they had read. None of them being the same because they were from different worlds but interestingly enough there were a lot of common themes. Kara sat in the bay window of Tealia's library enjoying the morning sun and remembering how she and Lina would pretend to be heroines from their favorite stories. She smiled, wishing Lina could see her now in her own real life adventure.

"This library is nothing compared to your father's." Tealia interrupted her musings. "I could get lost in his library for days, there's nothing like it."

"What is Eliada like?" Kara asked.

Alyne burst into the library before Tealia could answer. "Safiri's been seen on the outskirts of Alfsol." She announced. "The Sage says you must set off for Alverdene immediately Kara. Shaydon's getting the horses ready. I'm coming with you."

"I'm also coming," Tealia put her book down. "At least as far as Alverdene for now, I want to meet with the Elders."

"Is it safe for us to travel now?" Kara's skin prickled. "Safiri could be anywhere, waiting for the right moment to attack."

"A dozen Alfsol warriors have just arrived with the news. They'll accompany us for extra security. It sounds like Safiri only has one Themian with him," Alyne replied. "Plus, we have Shaydon...we're well protected."

Chapter Eight

Alverdene

By midmorning Kara, Shaydon, Alyne and Tealia were riding into the Cerulean Forest which boarded Evergreen and Alverdene. Although Kara was saddened to leave the tranquil pink skies of Evergreen she was also eager for the next part of her journey. The Alfsol warriors accompanied them discreetly, ensuring they were protected from all sides.

The trees in Cerulean were unusual in that they looked and smelt like Christmas trees, but had a bluish tint to them, making them quite exotic and different to any tree Kara had ever seen. She closed her eyes breathing in the pine and conifer aromas and listened to them whispering to each other. It sounded like she was back in Faylin and she was filled with a positive, uplifting energy, a sense of harmony and balance.

They rode in silence for a while until they came upon a hive of angry bees. Nobody was stung but the harmonious energy disappeared as the bees followed them, angrily buzzing around. Eventually they got used to the bees swarming around them, it didn't seem like they wanted to attack. They just buzzed and buzzed creating an irritable energy.

Tealia's turquoise eyes shone beautifully, enhanced by the bluish green of the trees and Kara noticed that

Shaydon could not take his eyes off her. Kara wondered why she felt a spark of jealousy. Tealia was beautiful and kind, a perfect match for Shaydon. Surely she should feel happy for him. She shook off the irksome feeling and brought her attention to what Tealia was saying.

"I love meeting with the Elders of Alverdene, they have so much wisdom to impart. The best stories are written in Alverdene, Kara. Although Arencia has some really good story tellers as well." Tealia waved the bees away from her grey mare's neck.

"The Elders have great power and influence within The Realm," said Shaydon. "Because they are such strong masters of expression, they are highly revered by the people."

"What do you mean by masters of expression?" Kara asked.

"When they talk, people listen. They have a great effect on people and are able to sway the masses with only the power of their words," Shaydon replied

"Oldwyn and Oldwina are the eldest of the Elders and they, together with my father, are Lord Eron's most trusted advisors." Tealia smiled as a bright blue butterfly flew around her. "So many from around The Realm travel to Alverdene to seek council."

"Trust you to bring up your father Tealia," Alyne said harshly and they all turned around to look at her in surprise. "Any chance to show off, we all know your father is the great and wise sage. So what? My father is a great warrior, Defender of The Realm! You don't hear me bragging about that every five minutes."

"Don't speak to Tealia like that!" Shaydon pulled aggressively on Elashe's reins.

"Don't tell me what to do! You think you are so strong and brave and invincible," Alyne sneered. "But deep down you know you will never measure up to our father, you're not half the warrior he is, and you never will be! You are way too selfish, always trying to prove yourself, seeking glory at whatever cost! How many years was I stuck as an eagle because of you!"

Both brother and sister glared at each other, an ugliness spreading across their features.

"You were transformed into an eagle because of your own ignorance and rash behaviour…. In fact, I preferred you as an eagle, I didn't have to baby sit you and suffer the consequences of your idiotic, spoilt, attention seeking."

"Why are you even here Shaydon?" Alyne spat. "You're supposed to get Kara safely home, but clearly that is not your priority! Why don't you just take off with Tealia as neither of you want to be here? You can't protect us if you are so distracted by *her*!"

"Alyne!" Tealia raised her voice. "That's unfair-"

"Stay out of it Tealia!" Kara found herself snapping.

Tealia's eyes turned icy as she stared hard at Kara. "Just who do you think you are?"

"I have no idea who I am!" Kara yelled and swung around accusingly at Shaydon. "I have no idea who I am because I've been lied to all my life!" She jumped off Boomer, dropped the reins and ran away from the path into the trees. She could hear the Alfsol warriors muttering in confusion and her friends calling her to come back and the bees buzzing. She had no idea where this anger had come from, but she felt righteous in it.

After a while she sat down and rested her back against an old tree closing her eyes. *What just happened?* She asked herself. She sat in silence for a short while until she heard footsteps approaching.

Shaydon wore a look of aggravation mingled with concern. "What's going on Kara?"

"Nothing," she bit her lip and turned away.

"I don't know what's got into you and Alyne."

Kara's throat hurt as she blinked back tears of rage. "Me and Alyne? What about you and Tealia? You haven't seen your sister in years and you say you are sworn to protect me and yet you only have eyes for your precious Tealia!" She leapt to her feet angrily. "I never realised how conceited you are, I bet you regret the day you found me because now you're stuck with me until you get rid of me in Eliada!"

Shaydon's eyes flashed. "That's not true!"

"I don't believe you!" Kara swatted away a bee. "In fact, don't worry, I don't want you to feel obligated to me in any way at all. I'll find my way. Take Tealia back to Evergreen and live happily ever after." She turned her back on him.

Shaydon grabbed her arm and swung her round to face him. "Kara don't you ever question my integrity or loyalty. How do you know what I want or don't want to do? Have you ever asked me? I choose to accompany you because I

101

want to. You've become like a sister to me … and our destinies are intertwined."

"Alyne is your sister and look how you just spoke to her, you see her as a brat and nuisance!"

Shaydon lowered his eyes in shame.

A movement in the nearby trees caught their attention and the forest darkened imperceptibly. They looked at each other and drew their swords. Shaydon held out his hand signalling to her to follow him quietly. The hairs on the back of Kara's neck stood up and she held her breath as she walked silently behind Shaydon. Suddenly a large owl flew out of the tree next to them hissing loudly, they both jumped and Kara fell backwards.

They heard a shout from the opposite direction. "Colonel! … My lady!" One of their guards ran up. "You need to come and see this!"

Shaydon cast a furtive glance back at the nearby trees before nodding curtly to the soldier. "Show us," He pulled Kara to her feet and they followed the guard back to the path.

Kara imagined she could smell wood burning some way off and kept squinting into the trees, adrenaline running through her. She half expected Safiri to leap out at any moment. As they got back to the group she shuddered with repulsion when she saw that two of the warriors were holding a Themian. It struggled and writhed in the grips of his captors, while cursing and wishing terrible things upon them, his long-forked tongue thrashing about.

"Death be upon youzz all." He sneered, "Anytime now you all will fall. Dizzasster awaits you four, leaving uzz The Realm and more, one by one you'll hate each other, turn your backs on one another." He eyed them all greedily.

Shaydon grabbed the toad by its throat which only infuriated the creature more and it spat out more curses and threats. Shaydon released him and snatched a small dagger from his boot, he then grabbed the toads long tongue with his free hand and brought the dagger down with his other and in one clean movement he sliced the creatures long forked tongue straight off. Everyone staggered back in horror. The warriors let go of the Themian and he fell to the ground clutching his throat and mouth, gagging and choking, evil tongue and voice gone.

"I'm sorry," Shaydon wiped his brow, "It spoke in evil rhyme, I couldn't let it continue."

"Good job brother," Alyne scowled at him, "how will we find out where Safiri is now, and what he's up to? This toad was more useful to us with his tongue." She kicked her heels into her horse angrily and rode ahead muttering and shaking her head.

Tealia put her hand on Shaydon's arm gently. "I think you were right to do that Shaydon, this is a very wicked creature."

She turned to Kara. "I'm so sorry Kara, I don't know what came over me."

"Me too," Kara said through tight lips. "I would like to ride alone for a while."

She mounted Boomer and followed Alyne whilst six of the warriors hastily went after them. She could hear

Shaydon instructing the rest of the warriors to tie up the Themian and keep him at a far distance from them. The buzzing bees had disappeared.

Kara realised that she had not had much time to herself in a long while. Having been raised as an only child she was used to spending time alone and she missed it. She felt confused and angry. Shaydon was her favorite person and she loved him dearly, why should she begrudge him happiness with Tealia. Tealia was good, kind and loving. They would be very happy together, but still, she could not shake off her anger at Shaydon nor the memory of Tealia's ice cold eyes and voice. Something stirred within her that made her feel uneasy. These were good people and she did not want to lose them. She brushed the hair out of her eyes feeling troubled.

The group rode through the rest of the forest in stony silence. Even the trees seemed to stop whispering as they passed. The forest eventually opened up onto a long clean white beach and a small shimmering blue sea which was exactly the same colour as the blue sky above. The sky and sea were separated by the mountains on the horizon.

Very tall pale people walked along the white sands. They were all dressed in white robes. Some seemed to be having choir practices in groups. Kara had never heard such beautiful voices. A few stood alone behind canvasses lost in their creations. An old couple wrote on long scrolls while a few others read silently from large ancient books. Some of the strange looking people appeared to be meditating and chanting soothing mantras. They all looked similar, white hair, sky blue eyes and blue throats. Kara stared in amazement. Every single one of them had a blue throat! She rubbed her eyes and blinked hard; she had not noticed the odd colouring initially.

The people of Alverdene returned their stares with great interest. The seemingly mutual interest turned to horror however when their eyes fell on the Themian prisoner. A dozen of the tallest Alverdenes soon approached the warriors and insisted on relieving them of the Themian. As they marched away with the captive the whole beach seemed to breathe a collective sigh of relief.

Soon after, they were led off the beach onto cobblestone streets winding their way through white Cycladic buildings. The weather was fine and Kara felt her airways open up. They were shown into a large building, where they were served iced peppermint spring water. It was so refreshing and seemed to cleanse the psychic debris of the harsh words spoken earlier. The four of them all looked around at each other, their expressions softened and shoulders loosened.

A very old man and woman entered the room, they also wore white robes. Their sky-blue eyes scanned the group intensely. Their throats were blue.

"It is a relief to see the air around you is beginning to clear." The old woman spoke clearly and articulately.

They all bowed their heads in reverence to the wise Elders.

The Elders greeted Tealia fondly before they turned their blue gaze on Shaydon and Alyne. "Master Shaydon and Mistress Alyne, you have been greatly missed. Your return brings renewed hope and joy to The Realm. We are eager to hear of your adventures on earth."

They embraced the brother and sister before focusing their intense gaze on Kara.

"My Lady Kara, I know you at once for your mother's eyes," Oldwyn had a rich deep clear voice.

Kara couldn't help thinking that he had the perfect bedtime story voice. "You knew my mother?"

"Yes we knew her," Oldwina stepped forward and took both of Kara's hands. "She was a wonderful person and she would be so proud of you. It is her bracelet you wear."

"I do?" Kara looked down at her bracelet. "I mean… I didn't know this belonged to her."

"You will learn more in time," Oldwina smiled knowingly. "I am sure you have many questions... as do we." She glanced at Shaydon and Alyne. "But first, let us eat, and then… it is important that we observe silence for an hour, so you may raise your levels of awareness and reconnect to your spirits."

"You have all been exposed to the slanderous vibration of a master manipulator," Oldwyn looked at each of them and they shivered under his scrutiny.

They followed the Elders out onto a large balcony overlooking the sea. A simple meal of wholesome fruits, vegetables and grains was set before them on a long wooden table. As they all sat down Kara learnt that the Elders of Alverdene ate a strictly vegetarian diet.

"We take great care of what passes in and out of our lips."

"And we take equally great care of what we feed our mind and soul."

Oldwyn prayed over the meal before he passed the platters around the table. "Our lives are built directly from our words, thoughts, beliefs and ideas which is why it is so important to take time throughout the day to observe silence and tune into divine spirit for direction."

"Turn inward rather than outward for advice." Oldwina dipped her bread in olive oil and vinegar. "After our meal you will each be taken to a solitary space where you may rest for an hour or so."

Oldwyn raised his glass and looked at each of them in turn once again. "Make a conscious effort in the quietness to notice and acknowledge what is good about the day."

Kara looked forward to the quiet time and happily followed another elder to a small garden with a fountain. The gentle running water relaxed her as she lay on a comfortable hammock and closed her eyes. At first her mind bumped and bounced around, bombarded with several different thoughts, but she forced herself to focus on her breathing and eventually her mind became still. In the quietness she remembered how grateful she was for Shaydon. She did not want to push him away. They had many happy memories together. He had suffered so much loss and heartbreak and now, after so many years, happiness had found him and instead of reconnecting with his family, he was here with her, making sure she got home safely, how could she deny him the love he had with Tealia? She would encourage their union.

Her mind strayed to her mother. The Elders seemed to know more about her than anyone else she had met thus far. She was determined to find out more. And what about her father... she sensed he was very close.

All too soon the elder came to collect her and took her to a pleasant courtyard. Tealia was already seated and she looked up happily as Kara entered. "Kara dear, come and sit next to me." She patted the chair to her right. "I'm sorry that I offended you in Cerulean. I was not myself."

Kara hugged her. "I'm sorry too. I don't know what came over us there."

"We hope your meditations were beneficial Kara and Tealia. You both appear to be calmer." Oldwyn and Oldwina entered the courtyard.

"I really needed it," Kara spoke truthfully. "I hope to make quiet time for myself more often."

"My heart has felt off balance since Cerulean," said Tealia. "The quiet has helped me to re-centre."

Shaydon and Alyne walked into the courtyard arm in arm, looking relieved and happy. Alyne walked straight up to Tealia. "I want only the best for my brother. I see how happy he is when he is with you and how much you care for each other. I would never stand in the way of love."

"Your blessing means the world, thank you Alyne." Tealia's eyes shone.

Alyne turned to Kara. "Don't doubt Shaydon's honour, nor his loyalty to you. He loves you as he loves me... and he would never betray either of us."

"I know," Kara smiled and looked up to Shaydon. "I'm ashamed that I ever doubted you, even for that short while.

You have been my rock, for as long as I can remember and I'm so grateful to have you in my life, for bringing me home, for staying with me even now when you should be making up for lost time with your family."

"You are also my family," Shaydon grinned and pulled Kara up into a big bear hug. He pulled Alyne in too. "My sister by birth and my sister by bond. I am bound to you both."

"Ahhh now that harmony and balance is restored," Oldwyn clapped his hands once. "May everyone please be seated."

"The Themian you found in the forest was responsible for your discord. He intended to divide you from each other so that you could be easily captured, one by one." Oldwina spoke.

Kara and Shaydon looked at each other. "Do you think Safiri was in Cerulean?"

"We believe so," Oldwyn answered. "But he did not expect his minion to get caught so quickly, he also had to take care being on Evergreen's boarder, he would not have wanted The Sage to be alerted. He has recently learned to fear The Sage."

"What we need to ascertain is how Safiri and his minions managed to enter into The Realm in the first place and how he roams our lands so freely now."

"His army was defeated in Alfsol," said Shaydon. "But some of them escaped."

"We will travel together to Onain shortly, in search of answers."

"But first we must tell you what we know of the Themians." Oldwina folded her hands in her lap.

"The Themians are not of the earth. They came from a small unseen planet, hidden in the dark depths of the universe." Oldwyn began. "They destroyed their own world and most of their race with their treacherous behavior. Turning on each other and using each other is their way of life. They are master manipulators and their slander and lies compromised the vibration and integrity of their world. They plotted and planned against themselves, backstabbing each other at every opportunity. Now they huddle together for protection, but they always keep one eye open as they are their own worst enemies."

"Masters of trickery and deceit, they took great joy in outwitting each other, only the most wicked survived," Oldwina shuddered. "One of the Universal Commandments is 'Thou shalt not bear false witness.' They lost their world but still continue to throw mean spirited words, which is the equivalent of spiritual assault."

"They are sly and greedy creatures, skilled in the corruption of psyches. That Themian tapped into each of your psyches as you traveled though Cerulean."

Oldwyn looked at Alyne. "The barren place where Safiri left you on earth is where the surviving Themians migrated when they destroyed their own world."

"Fortunately, Abellona found you and saved you from a terrible fate all those years ago." Oldwina spoke to Alyne, "she got to you before the Themians crawled out from under those rocks. They would have tried to undermine your belief in yourself, build doubts and turn you against your own kind."

"The Themians were looking for a way to take our Realm for themselves, they needed a new home. Their magic was dulled and weakened by the vibrations of earth... but it did not make them harmless by any means. They were still a dangerous breed. However, they needed a place like the Rainbow Realm where magic is naturally enhanced... there are places on earth where magic thrives, but the Themians were not adapting well there, they were dying out."

"Although Shaydon's behavior in Cerulean may have seemed barbaric, his instinct was right to cut off that creature's tongue." Oldwina's lips turned down in distaste. "The Themians' tongues are lethal."

"How did he tap into our psyches?" Kara asked.

"He corrupted the atmosphere of Cerulean by capturing a beehive and whispering dissonance amongst the bees before releasing them. The disturbed, angry energy of the bees spread, infecting your small group." Oldwina explained. "You remember the bees? He spread his negative intentions through them to get to you... now that was the effect of just one Themian, imagine their destruction in larger numbers."

"But your hearts are loyal and true, the effects were superficial." Oldwyn looked at them all in turn again. "Unfortunately, there are some beings, especially on earth, who do not know their own truth, they are easily swayed because they are unbalanced due to having no personal voice and these individuals may easily abandon loyalty and betray loved ones."

"Especially if they are seeking temporary approval and benefits, they will be more susceptible to manipulation," said Oldwina.

"Melia was manipulated by the Themians." Kara stated.

"Ah yes," Oldwyn leaned back in his chair frowning. "Melia's indiscretion."

"Melia has always been a wild card," said Oldwina, "we have often wondered whether she would take more from her father or her mother, she has taken traits from them both. Melia is very intelligent but her weakness lies in thinking she is cleverer than everyone, unfortunately in her attempts to manipulate, she cannot see that she in fact is being manipulated... and so her lack of discernment has lead her down dark paths at times, making her a prime target for the Themians."

"The Themians played to her vanity, told her what she wanted to hear, they gave her attention and behaved as a captivated audience, meanwhile they were luring her in, deceiving her. They used her to get the mask of deception into The Realm. Somehow the Themians are connected to Narcissa and together they planned to gain control and take over our Realm." Oldwyn told them.

There was another pause before Tealia spoke. "We must not judge Melia harshly, she thought she was in love with Safiri."

"She was just a pawn." Agreed Alyne.

"Melia's heart is true, although her vanity sometimes gets the better of her," said Oldwina. "Her mother's heart was true, her father was a vain glory seeker, he broke her mother's heart and very nearly destroyed her reign of Arencia."

"He was a self-serving ambitious young man who took advantage of his wife's love and loyalty to him," said Oldwyn sadly. "He was jealous of his wife's power and so she gave more and more of her power away to him, until there was barely anything left of her to give."

"It was a very sad situation for the family and Arencia was a miserable place to visit at that time." Oldwina continued. "The father became more and more addicted to unhealthy behaviours and crueler and more distant to his own family, seeking the pleasures of others. But before the end, their mother came to her senses and made things right in Arencia again."

"That is so sad," Kara thought out loud.

"That is why self-love is so important," Oldwina smiled, reaching up to pull a bunch of grapes from a dangling vine above her. "It is not selfish to love oneself and take care of oneself, when we each accept that we are responsible for our own happiness in life, then we will not cling to one another. Trying to please someone for fear of losing them is not love. Giving away our power is not love. Living a fulfilling life is an honest way to live, I hope in time you will all understand these words."

"Melia knows she made a mistake," said Kara after a while. "She admitted it. It is in the past."

Oldwyn nodded his head. "While we must acknowledge the past so that we may learn from it, we must also not give the past power, getting stuck there only creates more misery."

"You must know that although the discord in Cerulean was manipulated, there is nothing inappropriate about having feelings and expressing them." Oldwina passed the bunch of grapes around. "When a person can bravely speak their truth without injury or disrespect they have the power to create a better life for themselves."

Oldwyn looked at Kara directly. "Kara if there is anything you learn here today; I hope it will be the power your words have to create your life. It is something we discuss with all our guests, so your friends have heard this before. Your subconscious is programmed to accept all that you suggest to it. You may have been subjected to the beliefs of your guardians on earth, but you have the ability to reprogram those beliefs by using the two powerful words 'I am' you affirm and create who you want to be by choosing the words that follow. Constantly affirm you are who you want to be and you will soon become it."

Just then Jarita flew into the courtyard and gently landed on Alyne's shoulder nudging her ear softly.

Alyne was delighted. "I can still understand her!" She stroked Jarita's copper feathers listening intently. "The princesses of Arencia send their regards...There are still some Dark Ones spreading fear in the lower regions but The Sage has cast a light of love down and the people are responding well. It is under control for now... They wish us well on our quest... Jarita has spotted Safiri lurking amongst the higher regions… It appears the Dark Ones are unable to pass beyond Alfsol so Safiri is alone for now."

Jarita flew to Kara's shoulder.

"Your father Lord Eron requests that you set out for Onain without delay," Alyne told Kara. "He is waiting to meet with us in Eliada."

Kara felt excitement welling up within her, her father was calling her. This was the first acknowledgment she had received from him. She was going to reunite with him soon. *I am… a worthy daughter of the Rainbow Realm,* she affirmed to herself silently.

Oldwyn stood up. "We will rest now and start off for Onain early tomorrow morning."

Chapter Nine

Onain

After a light breakfast, the group of friends set out for Onain accompanied by Oldwyn, Oldwina and the Alfsol guards. The mountain paths were narrow allowing two horses breadth only and so they rode in pairs. Shaydon and Kara rode together.

"Did you notice how the Alverdene skies barely darkened? Even while we slept last night, the sky was light blue," Shaydon looked up at the clouds. "The Onain skies, in contrast, remain a deep midnight blue, whatever time of day it is."

"Isn't that unsettling?"

"Onain has a haunting, mysterious quality, and yet it's beautiful and tranquil at the same time. You won't find people there. Anyone can pass through Onain as they wish but very few can lift the veil and enter the Garden of Illumination. The Sage, the Elders and your father have the powers to do so and they can invite others to join them."

Elash and Boomer walked comfortably neck by neck, ears twitching. "We must make the most of this visit Kara, it's a rare opportunity to look into the waters of Onain. Very few people have ever done so. The visions presented can easily be misinterpreted, even by our wise ones at times, so care is needed when drawing conclusions."

Shaydon pulled on Elash's reins to let Boomer pass in front of him as the path narrowed, forcing the horses to continue in single file for some time.

The further they rode, the darker the sky became, deepening into an indigo blue and stars became visible, twinkling against the dark background. The full moon that was unique to Onain lit their way. Kara knew it could only be mid-morning and rode along quietly awed by the change of skies. Nobody spoke, but each person's aura became vividly prominent in the dark surroundings. A whitish blue aura emanated from Oldwyn and Oldwina while the warm golden Alfsol light lit up the warriors, Shaydon and Alyne. Tealia was bathed in a soft green shimmer. Kara looked down at herself wondering if her aura showed or not. The path widened slightly and Oldwina steadied her horse and waited for Kara to ride alongside her.

"You do have a light Kara, a pure white energy protects you," Oldwina answered her unspoken question. "Aura colours can change. When a person finds their purpose and carves their niche in their world, then the aura's colour will become somewhat permanent."

They continued to ride on in silence, deeper into the mystical region of Onain. The ground and surroundings levelled out and Kara became aware of soft white mists and orbs floating gently about in the dark air. There were large pools of water which reflected the stars and moon upon their glassy surfaces, exaggerating the chill in the atmosphere and Kara shivered feeling something more than the cold.

They came upon a wide veil of mist. Here Oldwyn instructed them to dismount and leave their horses with the Alfsol guards. He parted the mist as if he were drawing open curtains and stood aside for them to pass through. There, behind the veil, was the overgrown but enchanting Garden of Illumination. A few floating flames provided soft subtle light. Several stone chalices were placed around the garden. The chalices were filled with water. At the furthest end of the garden was an enormous round table-like basin also filled with water.

The Elders beckoned the four friends to it. Orbs and creatures of mist drifted about in the softly lit garden, circling enigmatically around the chalices and overgrown vines. Some hovered silently above them in the air. Kara felt as though she was being intensely watched, but she felt no fear, just a strange curiosity.

When they were all gathered around the large table basin Oldwyn spoke.

"Here in the land of Onain we are blessed with the gift of insight, hindsight and foresight. These waters show us visions of what has been, what is now and what may come to pass." He gently laid his hands on the stone rim. "We have an opportunity now to look deeper into circumstances as well as individuals. We hope to accurately assess the situation and come up with a long-lasting solution."

"We wish to see how Safiri is roaming our lands so freely." Oldwina spoke clearly as her gaze swept around the table basin. "We all need to make this our clear, collective intention before we look into these waters, it is important that we all share the same intention otherwise the visions we receive may be confusing and distorted. Please, take a moment to clear your minds and focus on our collective intention."

After some minutes had passed Oldwyn cleared his throat.

"Are we ready?" He asked.

Everyone nodded solemnly.

"Very well, I will say a prayer now, please keep your minds on our intention. Upon conclusion of the prayer we should all focus deeply into the water before us. And if our intentions are pure, we should all receive the same visions."

The water began to swirl as a heavy mist rose from the great basin. They all focused deeply into the water. The water eventually stilled and large boulders and rocks appeared in its depths, the vision took them into an opening inside the rocks displaying a large cave. Therein were about thirty Themians of various ages and sizes. Loud hissing and spitting sounds were heard. A Themian, somewhat taller and slimmer than the rest rose to stand before the squat Themian who Kara recognised from the battle at Alfsol. This squat fat Themian was the same who had attacked her in the fort, the very same Themian she had destroyed.

The tall Themian spoke. "Slyne why do you do this to me?"

"The only reason you wazz spared, wazz not because we all cared. No Narcissa, not at all, we killed your useless parents, cause they couldn't rule, but their ancient leaderzz blood runs in your veinzz,so now it's only you what can survive these painzz. You alone can withstand the transformation and then you will bring uzz our salvation." Slyne the large toad spoke.

Kara realised Slyne must have been the leader for when she addressed the crowd, they immediately became silent. "It izz time for Narcissa to repay our mercy. Into this pot she'll go, you'll see. She may live, she may die, we have to try. Our powerzz weaken every day, the longer we stay on earth the more we waste away. We Themians won't survive much longer, we need The Realm to make uzz stronger." She shifted her eyes slyly around the cave. "Now each of uzz hazz to sacrifice our blood, for this concoction to work it must be thick azz mud. Some of uzz are old and weary and will not survive the loss of blood, you'll see. But it matters not, their remainzz will go to the pot." Slyne narrowed her bulging eyes in warning. "If anyone darezz to disagree with me, we'll curse them to infinity, they'll be sliced right through the gut and their dirt will go in the pot. For the cauzze!" She shouted at last.

"For the cauzze!" Most of the Themians buzzed in agreement, the words echoing off the cave walls.

Slyne turned back to Narcissa. "If the transformation should succeed, you'll have great powerzz indeed. Men will fall at your feet, you will be able to seduce any man you meet. The Realm's strength liezz in Alfsol, get to Commander Caine and you will have control."

The vision zoomed in on a large cauldron from where the hissing and spitting sounds were coming. Strange looking objects and various animal parts melted into the thick boiling concoction. One by one the Themians stepped hesitantly towards Slyne and held their arms over the bubbling cauldron. Slyne sliced viciously across each arm using a dagger, ignoring their cries of agony and grinning gleefully as their black blood flowed from the cuts into the cauldron. Slyne's assistant pushed away each Themian after the assault, making space for the next victim. As Slyne had predicted, this process was too much for some of the older Themians who disintegrated into dust as their arms were sliced open, when this happened she cackled gleefully scooping up their dusty remains and tossing them into the potion. "Good, good, their powerzz are locked into the potion… for the cauzze!" After the last Themian had been cut she began to chant in a strange buzzing language and the others joined in, the buzzing became louder and more irritating as the tall young Themian from earlier was dragged towards the cauldron, looking terrified.

"Wait!" She cried. "what if this kills me?"

"There izz no other way," Slyne smacked her lips in anticipation. "You have the ancient leaders' blood Narcissa!"

The young Themian was thrown into the cauldron, her blood curdling screams died away as she slowly disappeared into the boiling potion.

Several minutes passed.

"She's dead," murmurs came from the Themians. "We are doomed now, curse her."

"Our last hope izz gone."

Slyne raised her fat reptile-like limb. "Quiet!" She commanded, peering into the cauldron, "somethings happening in there…"

She leapt back as the cauldron cracked loudly, then suddenly exploded. A beautiful young woman slowly uncurled and stood up from the remains. She had dark skin, long platinum hair and ice-cold blue eyes, she looked down at herself in gradual appreciation and a cruel smile began to form on her perfect lips.

"Show me!" She demanded

A small Themian stepped forward in awe with a large broken mirror which the woman snatched from him.

She viewed herself in the mirror admiringly, her eyes glinting. "See how beautiful I am, see how powerful I am." Her voice rose clearly with each word, no trace of a buzz nor rhyme.

Suddenly she flung her arm out and grabbed the squat Slyne by her throat, she lifted her off her feet, glaring at her. "Change is upon us, I will take back leadership of our people as my ancestors did before me. It is I who will ensure the defeat of the Rainbow Realm for our kind. Once we have seized The Realm the Themians shall grow, prosper and rule supreme under *my* reign! Are we clear?"

The Themians applauded loudly in agreement and the old Slyne was dropped unceremoniously to the ground....

Narcissa bent over her and spoke coldly. "Know this Aunt Slyne... I will take your God forsaken life if ever you try to deceive me in anyway... it will be the last action you ever take. You have done well to make me the most powerful Themian alive, and I will spare you for now but beware that you do not meet the same evil fate you bestowed upon my parents." The image darkened, the waters swirled and the mist rose again.

When the mist cleared they were looking into a small room. The newly transformed and beautiful Narcissa was seated on a wooden chair whilst a little man served her a drink. As the little man turned around, the image zoomed in on his face, Kara heard a collective gasp from her companions before recognising the little man as Fergus, Keeper of the Gate.

Fergus shook his head. "I don't know will it work, Narcissa."

"It will work and you will be well rewarded." Narcissa sipped her drink narrowing her eyes seductively at him.

"Ye've promised me Sanguinavia and control of all the mines to be sure," Fergus nodded. "But is it really worth it for me to be involving meself in such shenanigans."

"You can have Arencia as well," she smiled slyly. "The princesses of Arencia will be at your sole disposal."

"This will all be taking some time, sure you know yourself." Fergus rubbed his hands together greedily. "But I trust you'll be making it worth me while sure. You'll be needing me after all, cannot be done without my help, not at all."

The waters swirled yet again taking them into the warm sunny region of Alfsol, into a large poppy field where Narcissa was dressed in a bridal gown, walking hand in hand with a handsome warrior who Kara thought to be Commander Caine. He stared lovingly at Narcissa almost in disbelief that he had married someone so desirable.

The image remained for a few seconds only, before swirling frantically and opening into a large home, running along a corridor, down some steps into a dark underground room where a young boy stood biting back tears as Narcissa bent over him scolding. "You should be ashamed of yourself Safiri, what did I ever do to deserve such a useless and incompetent son as you, you will stay in here until you deserve to be in my presence." She climbed the stairs muttering cruel insults, as she got to the door she repeated loudly. "Useless, incompetent, shameful!" She slammed the door and locked it behind her.

The waters changed yet again taking them into a field of sunflowers. The same boy was there, slightly older. Narcissa was embracing him and stroking his hair. "There now Safiri, you mustn't make me angry. I love you only when you do as I say, you have done well this time." She smiled icily as she looked upon the burning corpse of a small creature.

The waters darkened and mist rose as an image opened again on Narcissa shrieking at an adolescent Safiri. "You have failed me once again! How can a mother love such an incompetent son? Get out of my sight! I don't ever want to see you again!" She picked up a vase and threw it at him in frustration.

Safiri ducked and the vase smashed against the wall behind him. "But father says-"

"I don't give a damn what your useless father says!" Narcissa spat. "Mark my words, his precious Realm will crumble, just be strong Safiri and choose the right side!"

The waters swirled violently again this time splashing its audience, it cleared after a few moments opening on the Themians in the cave.

"She hazz tricked uzz." An elderly Themian spoke to the old squat Slyne. "Narcissa keeps The Realm all to herself while we sit here waiting to die, she tricked uzz with a nasty lie!" He slammed his fist sideways against the rough rock wall.

"Patience my friend, we don't trust her but it's not the end." Slyne cocked her head. "She hazz the greed for power she does but she can't rule over anyone without uzz. I have newzz from her accomplice… Master Fergus."

"What newzz?"

"The princess of Arencia will be tricked into coming here." She smacked her lips together greedily. "We are preparing a mask of deceit which we'll lay at Melia's feet. She izz selfish and vain but her trust we must gain. We'll tell Melia what she wants to hear and then we'll gift her the magic mask, Safiri will then take up the task."

"There izz not enough power amongst uzz here, to make such a mask will destroy most of uzz I fear."

"Yes to magic a mask will take sacrifice, but we have enough power left and the strongest of uzz will rise."

"Too many we have sacrificed for this cause, your plan Slyne izz full of flaws. What can a handful of Themians do? Even if we get into The Realm, we are too few."

"Ohh we aren't the only onezz working for this cause, a massive army is preparing to storm Lord Eron's doorzz. Over this army we will rule, do you think me a complete fool?"

"And how many of uzz will you be taking in the making of this mask? Who of uzz will you kill for the task?"

"Not too many, see behind you in that small pot what cooks. We already started preparing, your names are in my books."

The elderly Themian turned in horror to look at the small cauldron on the fire behind him. Slyne took the opportunity to stab her ugly dagger into his back, he gasped in disbelief before disintegrating into a pile of dust. The old leader scooped up his remains before they disappeared and tossed them into the cauldron gleefully.

"Not so many needed now izz there," she cackled. "The mask izz almost done, aren't I such a clever one, hee hee hee hee."

Once again the vision clouded over and the water began to swirl. When it cleared it was back in the rocks but out in the open and not in a cave. There stood Safiri as Kara knew him, he was staring out in the distance, a look of hunger in his eyes. Fergus stood behind him.

Safiri turned to Fergus. "You are sure the main portal has opened?"

"It has." The little man wrung his hands.

"You have been gone all these years, I thought you were trapped within The Realm?" Safiri's eyes narrowed on Fergus.

"I was, and The Realm folk were thinking as I was trapped here on earth."

"No one from The Realm ever saw you?"

"They did not. I have the powers of teleporting on me I do, as do you and your kind." Fergus gestured to the cave behind them. "I also have the powers of invisibility on me I do… but you'll be after knowing where you can teleport and where you can't in The Realm... And that's where I can be helping yourselves, as long as the arrangement between me and your mam still stands." He eyed Safiri beadily.

Safiri looked him up and down with a degree of contempt. "I stand by my mother's arrangement with you."

"Sure I had some help from your wee mask all these years past," Fergus smiled slyly.

Safiri's eyes widened. "You have my mask?" He stepped menacingly closer to Fergus.

"I'm holding it now sure." Fergus said nonchalantly as he put his hand inside his shirt and pulled out the mask. "Sure didn't I find it after you dropped it making away with Lord Eron's bairn...and didn't I pick it up during all those shenanigans way back. I'd be keeping it safe for yerself sure."

Safiri snatched the mask from Fergus and stared at it possessively.

"The only thing is, see." Fergus sat down cross legged on the rocks. "You'll be needing to give that mask to one of your kind will ye not, because when I'm about gallivanting with yourselves in The Realm, who'll be after keepin' the gate? We'll be needing one of yours to impersonate me, we will."

"Yes," Safiri agreed reluctantly, "unfortunately we will have to leave the mask, the Gate to the portal is a key position and to have one of ours there is of utmost value... but... we will have to distract that tiresome Xylia and her forest creatures somehow."

"That'll be easy enough sure." Fergus picked his nose thoughtfully, "you'll have raised up another army again?"

"Yes" Safiri looked down on him. "It is amazing how many vile creatures can be found in the cracks and crevices of this earth, and how many have had their eyes on The Realm for eons."

"Lost ones have always coveted The Realm... they have," said Fergus. "Speaking of lost ones, you'll be eager to know that Kara Gabriel has surfaced she has."

Safiri grabbed Fergus and raised him off his feet. "Where is she? Tell me now!"

"Calm yourself man and put me down sure!"

"Tell me!" Safiri shook him.

"Well, sure Shaydon will be taking her straight to The Realm won't he."

"Shaydon," Safiri laughed and dropped Fergus to the ground. "He came after me, thinking he could defeat me. The only reason I've allowed him to live is that I knew he may lead me to Kara or his sister Alyne. They could both have been of some use, but that Xylia has hidden Shaydon from me for some time now as well."

"I wouldn't be underestimating Master Shaydon were I you Safiri."

Safiri swatted at a fly ignoring the warning. "We have the powers of teleportation but once we are within The Realm, teleporting is not always possible, could even get us killed."

"I've been workin' on this issue, I have... you'll see." Fergus grinned. "I know all the weak spots and have worked tunnels through, I have. I've created teleportals too, not just a pretty face am I!"

"The fort of Alfsol?"

"I know how to get in I do, there's a wee weak spot under the moat. I'll show ye sure."

"And the higher regions. I need to get in there?"

"You will, I'll show ye."

"Do you know how to break into The Purge?" Safiri leaned close towards Fergus.

"Sure I do now."

"I thought Lord Eron was the only one able to free prisoners from that hell."

"Sure if he's alive but if ye think of killing Lord Eron, The Purge will be vulnerable and once he's dead, I'll know what to do sure, we'll get your mam out, we will."

"We won't stop at freeing my mother. I want to free all of the souls imprisoned there." Safiri's eyes glowed red with ambition.

The waters swirled and then went blank and still. No more visions came forth.

Some time passed as they continued to stare into the motionless water. Eventually Oldwina spoke. "We have seen much and are grateful for these revelations, there is no more to see at this time."

"Much has been revealed indeed." Oldwyn gazed into the distance. "Narcissa is a Themian. And when they transformed her in that dark potion, her powers were greatly enhanced. The Themians sacrificed a lot of their collective power for her."

"Their race was dwindling," Oldwina said. "They became distressed at the amount of time it was taking Narcissa to accomplish her mission, they needed entrance into our world where their magic would be strong... but because they were dying out with very few remaining they needed to join forces with Dark Ones and others like them to form an army."

"Their powers were limited on earth," Oldwyn stepped back from the basin.

"Yes," Oldwina followed. "There are enchanted areas on earth where powerful magic is permitted but these places are highly protected by the guardians of the earth...the guardians are strong and very little gets by them."

"Like Faylin, which Xylia protects fiercely," Shaydon looked deeply into the water hoping to seek more answers. "So, we've established that Safiri is half Themian because his mother was a Themian, and he has inherited some of their abilities, like teleporting."

"Indeed." Oldwina moved closer to Shaydon and gently put her hand under his chin turning his face away from the water. "But he is much stronger than the Themians because they transferred most of their powers to his mother, and she would have passed them down to him, albeit unknowingly, through birth."

Oldwyn looked thoughtfully up at the mists circling above them. "Safiri has more greed than Narcissa, for freeing The Purge would ensure him a dark and powerful army... allowing him easier access to worlds beyond our

Realm… Narcissa's ambition was to take over The Realm. Safiri wants The Realm and more."

"Is my father in danger?" Kara remembered Safiri's glowing red eyes.

"Your father is very powerful." Oldwyn put his hand on Kara's shoulder. "I don't know how Safiri, or Fergus for that matter, can even imagine an attempt on his life. I feel their ambition will be their downfall before the end."

"Safiri is able to burst into flame because the Alfsol light he inherited from his father has been crossed with the Themian dark, magical powers of Narcissa." Oldwina walked thoughtfully around the basin. "Creating an immensely powerful, arrogant being. We know that, without the mask, he can no longer disguise himself and he cannot become invisible, but… he can teleport and because he is in cahoots with Fergus, Keeper of the Gate, he has access to several illegal portals within The Realm and knowledge of all the vulnerable areas in our strongholds."

"That explains how they got into the Alfsol fort." Shaydon frowned. "Even I didn't know there was a weak area beneath the moat."

"We must send word immediately to the lower regions and Xylia." Oldwyn made for the veil of mist. "They must be warned that there is an imposter at the gate. Xylia probably believes that Fergus was overpowered again meanwhile the enemy has been using the mask at will, allowing free entrance for all."

"Fergus has been very busy betraying our world these past thirteen years, more than thirteen years." Shaydon said angrily. "How many tunnels and teleportals has he built over the years, weakening our Realm just so he can have the mines. Greedy little beast!" His fists clenched. "I can't wait to get my hands on him."

"Fergus is the biggest disappointment of all," agreed Alyne. "But right now, Safiri is our greatest threat. We have to focus on bringing him down."

"We will wait here while Oldwyn sends word." Oldwina smiled at them. "You can take advantage of these extra moments to look into the smaller chalices if you so wish, for your personal queries."

One by one Kara watched each of her friends go to separate chalices. They all paused momentarily before they bent to look into the visionary waters. She looked around for Oldwina and spied her by a chalice set in a little nook, Oldwina beckoned to her. "Come Kara, what do you wish to know?"

"I've so many things I want to ask," Kara said quietly. "I don't know where to begin."

"It's alright, you will be alone with this vision, let the waters show you what they will." Oldwina pointed into the chalice. "Take a look, I am right here if you need me."

Kara paused by the basin to say a small silent prayer and then bent to look into the waters. It was different to the large table basin, she momentarily felt like she was being pulled in as the water stirred and the mist rose, but she held on tightly to the rim of the chalice and dug her heels into the ground. As the pulling sensation passed a garden appeared in the depths of the water, a woman sat on a bench under a tree which had creepers of purple flowers cascading from it. The woman was cradling a baby, she turned her gaze away from the baby and looked straight into Kara's eyes. Kara gasped for she knew the woman could see her too. For a split second she thought she was looking at her own reflection because she stared into golden brown eyes just like hers, but these eyes were older and wiser. Kara realised this woman must be her mother, as a great warmth filled her heart. They stared at each other intently, drinking in the sight of each other. Then her mother smiled warmly at her and they both looked back to the baby who was playing with the same crystal bracelet Kara wore.

"How?"

"We don't have much time my darling Kara," her mother interrupted gently. "I have missed you so, the waters will only give us a few seconds... remember your dream... remember the rain... you have the power."

The water started swirling rapidly.

"Wait!" Kara cried desperately, but the vision had already changed and as it cleared, she found herself back in the cottage at the edge of Faylin. She saw her younger self sitting at the kitchen table in a memory with Maja and Dajo.

"Women must know their place," Dajo was saying. "A woman belongs at home, as long as she takes care of the home, cooks, cleans, bears children, she'll be looked after by her husband. She must mind her manners and take care of her appearance." He looked pointedly at Maja before turning back to Kara. "I have no doubt you will make someone a fine wife one day Kara."

"Always be accommodating and pleasant." Maja agreed, looking more disheveled than usual, breaking green beans into a bowl. "The world can be a difficult place for a woman, you'll catch more flies with honey than with vinegar and we all need to have a man we can count on."

"Not all men can be counted on," Kara retorted.

"So you think you can count on yourself?" Dajo snorted derisively. "You'll end up an old maid with that attitude and that will be a big problem for you, but don't worry, I'll ensure you'll always be taken care of."

Kara felt a deadening sensation in the pit of her stomach, she looked at Maja sadly as the water swirled again, then she felt a hand on her shoulder gently pulling her back. She looked round to find Oldwina watching her intently.

"Oldwyn will be here any minute now Kara and I wish to speak with you privately." Oldwina looked at her sympathetically. "As children, we are dependent on our caretakers, not only for physical safety and affection, but psychic well-being as well. If we are taught that in order to be loved, we must be other than ourselves, we do so, but at a grave cost. Our self-worth should not be dependent upon our appearance only, although there is nothing wrong with taking care of our appearance. Our self-worth should be dependent upon our creativity, our spirituality, our mental capacity and our ability to contribute to our world." Oldwina placed both hands on Kara's shoulders and looked deeply into her eyes. "It is time for you to discover your true self, Kara. Start by looking for the gifts that come disguised in loss and frustration, this offsets the tendency to feel like a victim and give away power, focus on opportunities to grow and evolve as a spiritual being." She released Kara's shoulders as Oldwyn entered the garden.

Chapter Ten

Eliada

They were soon mounted on their horses and traveling through the higher mountain ranges of The Realm. The further away from Onain they traveled the lighter the skies became, fading into a soft lilac background against the snow-capped mountains. The Alfsol warriors were with them still, Oldwyn, Oldwina and Shaydon rode ahead out of hearing range.

Tealia's turquoise eyes sparkled with excitement as she told Kara and Alyne about her personal vision in the waters of Onain. "I was standing wrapped in Shaydon's arms in a field of sunflowers." She smiled wistfully. "A child appeared from under a clump of the large flowers teasing us, Shaydon picked him up and swung him in the air while two more children ran towards us giggling, a gorgeous little girl ran into my arms while the other little boy pounced on Shaydon." She sighed dreamily. "Now I know we are meant to be together because we are destined to marry and have a family."

"That's wonderful for you and Shaydon." Alyne tried to smile but there was a shadow in her eyes.

"I know it was risky for me to ask about the future, because the future is not promised and can change." Tealia stroked her mare's neck, "but this image was crystal clear, I can't help but believe it to be true."

"Anyone can see that you and Shaydon are besotted with each other. One day you *will* make a beautiful family." Kara smiled encouragingly before turning to Alyne. "Are you going to tell us what you saw Alyne?"

"I also asked to see the future, but I didn't receive a clear vision, the waters were murky and troubled.... I was looking for my father, but I couldn't find him." Alyne's voice trembled slightly. "I wish I hadn't looked into the waters."

"I'm sorry Alyne," Tealia said. "Sometimes the waters of Onain won't show anything, visions aren't always guaranteed."

"I have been away so long all I wanted was to return home… and now that I'm here, so much has changed… or maybe it hasn't changed, but I have," Alyne shrugged. "I still feel lost sometimes… I miss the exhilaration of soaring through the air… although I was trapped in the form of an eagle, I had never felt so free." She looked up at the clouds wistfully.

They rode on in silence, breathing in the crisp mountain air, listening to the horses' hooves plodding softly on the earth, the clear lilac sky painted a peaceful scene, but Kara empathised with Alyne's disquiet. Kara had left the only home she remembered, and although she had never quite felt like she belonged there, there wasn't much expected from her which gave her a comfort and freedom. Here she felt that people had high expectations of her and she wasn't sure she could live up to being 'Lord Eron's daughter.' At times she also felt lost in this land that was her rightful home… she was excited to meet her father but nervous and anxious at the same time.

"Kara… Kara?" Alyne was speaking to her. "You are miles away."

"I'm sorry, did you say something?" Kara brushed her hair out of her eyes.

"Did you see anything in the waters of Onain?"

Kara told them about her vision of her mother.

Tealia's eyes widened. "Really Kara, that's incredible!"

"Your mother spoke to you?" Alyne was also surprised. "Did you tell Oldwina about this?"

"We only spoke about Maja and Dajo," Kara bit her lip. "I think Oldwina saw the reflection of my guardians but not the image with my mother. I can't say for sure, but she didn't speak of it."

"Your mother gave you a message… you must take heed of her words… what dream did she speak of?" Tealia asked.

"And why would she stress the importance of rain?"

Kara told them about the dream she had experienced in Sanguinavia and how she had called on rain to extinguish Safiri's fire. As she spoke Kara realised that she had not dreamt of Safiri since that time.

Alyne and Tealia looked at each other and back to Kara in confusion.

"Well, it won't be long before we reach Eliada, if anyone has the answers it will be Lord Eron." Alyne pointed up as they rode around a sharp bend and the view of a magnificent large city appeared some distance ahead of them.

The city was built of church like palatial white buildings which shimmered as a mirage in a violet white aura. Kara gasped at the splendid sight of her home and felt an intense urge to gallop up the rest of the way. However, there was still some distance to go and the path was steep in places as it ascended. Gradually the way became level and easier for both riders and horses. With some relief they reached a large plateau, not far from the city of Eliada. The Elders and Shaydon waited for them to catch up. To the right of the plateau a stream filled with purple lotus flowers trickled past them and to the left was an area of tall Ficus trees.

Oldwyn instructed them to dismount from the horses and let the Alfsol warriors continue on the path up to Eliada. "There is a passage through these Ficus trees I wish us to take," he said mysteriously.

They walked through the quiet trees for a while, no sounds were made here unlike the other forests Kara had been in, this place was completely silent. Oldwyn stopped suddenly and held out his hand signalling to them to follow suit. He beckoned to Kara, she went to him and looked where he was pointing. There was a small clearing in the trees and bright light shone down into it. There sat a man cross legged, he was not seated on the ground however, but had levitated at least a foot above the ground his hands resting in his lap, palms up. He wore a long violet cloak which billowed gently behind him in the quiet breeze. His eyes were closed. Kara stared unblinkingly, taking in every detail of him. His medium length jet black hair was streaked with thick lines of silver. A violet white glow radiated around his head like a halo. Although his face rested in a peaceful pose, he had a distinguished powerful look, his strong jaw line contrasted with his soft long black lashes which rested calmly on his high cheek bones. Suddenly… his eyes opened and he stared straight at Kara with dazzling violet eyes.

Kara gasped as he rose slowly out of his seated position. They did not take their eyes off each other and Kara found herself walking in a trance towards him as he walked towards her. Both being drawn to each other, they met in the middle of the clearing and she fell into his arms without hesitation. A profound sense of well-being and safety wrapped around itself her. Her deepest doubts and fragile feelings disappeared in that moment. She knew that everything was going to be alright and this was where she was meant to be. Tears fell softly down her cheeks; she did not want this moment to end. They held each other for several long minutes.

Eventually she took a deep breath and stepped back, looking up into her father's deep violet eyes. He smiled down at her. "Welcome home daughter." His voice was velvety and rich.

Kara found she could not speak, there was so much she wanted to say and ask but words seemed inadequate in this moment.

"I have been waiting for you Kara, ever since the day you were taken away, I have waited for this moment."

She found her voice at last. "Father, why did you not come to find me?"

"The portal between our worlds was closed. The way was blocked, I knew it would open when the time was right."

"Why didn't you come to meet me once I was in The Realm?"

"It was part of your soul's journey to find your way home. All of life with its challenges and relationships makes perfect sense to our souls, everything exists for the purpose of our growth. I had no right to interfere with your journey, as much as I longed too, my daughter. This has been one of your most important experiences, I would have done you a disservice had I intervened. You have met soul mates along the way who you will cherish for lifetimes. I have waited for you to make your way back to me whilst you have been learning valuable lessons in the process....it is destiny that we reunite at this time, in this way."

"I don't understand," Kara shook her head.

"You will understand... in time." Lord Eron's eye glittered in the light. "We have much to share with each other. To learn from one another. Earth is a fascinating world. I looked upon you often in the waters of Onain, I watched you grow from afar and I look forward to hearing of your experiences there."

He looked away to her companions and smiled encouragingly at them, beckoning them forth.

They all came before him and bowed reverently. He greeted each of them warmly by name.

"Shaydon, you have done well, son of Alfsol. You have grown into a man of great honour and integrity, with a bright and successful future ahead of you." Eron bowed his head respectfully before shaking Shaydon's hand. "I rested easily knowing you had taken Kara under your protection. I am in deep gratitude to you for bringing her home, for keeping her safe and guiding her in her vulnerable years on earth."

Eron turned to Alyne. "Alyne, you have returned with the gift of an eagle's perspective. You have endured enough trials to appreciate this gift... I trust you will use this power wisely." He placed one hand on Alyne's shoulder and the other on Shaydon's. "It is with great pride that I welcome you both home. You will both be awarded positions of high honour in The Realm." Lord Eron then took both of Alyne's hands into his own and lowered his voice. "I knew your mother would recover on your return, you are no longer lost, it may take some time for you to adjust, be patient with yourself."

His expression darkened slightly as he addressed the Elders. "My trusted friends, Oldwyn and Oldwina. A darkness lies nearby. Our beloved Realm has been corrupted. But together we will prevail, as we always have."

His face softened as he put his hand over his heart to address Tealia. "Welcome Tealia, a daughter of Evergreen is always a joy to behold. It pleases me to know you have befriended Kara. You will council her well, as your father councils me. I am deeply grateful to The Sage for his involvement in the recent battle. Safiri underestimated your father, it seems that he continues to underestimate the powers and laws we hold within our Realm as well as the loyalty between our regions."

He took hold of Kara's hand. "Come now, if it pleases those of you who cannot teleport, to rest your hands upon my cloak, I will be able to teleport you into Eliada. Commander Aldridge awaits us."

"My father is in Eliada?" Alyne was surprised.

"Of course." Lord Eron smiled and held out his other hand to Alyne. "A battle hangs in the air and so we are in need of our greatest Commander."

Kara felt a tugging sensation in her belly just then and her body lifted from the ground spinning her around in a vortex of air until her feet landed gently on soft grass not far from a small pond, also filled with lotus flowers. They stood before a large shimmering palace where Commander Aldridge was waiting for them. He looked relaxed and happy, not like a man expecting battle and was not even wearing armour, only a sword hung from his belt. Alyne ran joyfully into his embrace.

"Aldridge my good man," said Eron. "It brings me great pleasure to see you so happy, it has been a long time coming. What joyful news of Katran's recovery and our children's return. I am aware that Safiri lurks nearby but let that not distract us from these blessed reunions. Go now and spend some time with Shaydon and Alyne while I do the same with Kara."

"Thank you Lord Eron, these last few days have been the happiest of my life, may I say what a pleasure it is to witness you also reunite with your daughter," Aldridge smiled.

"Blessed are we Aldridge, to be here for their return." Eron nodded before turning to Tealia and the Elders.

"The Sage will join us shortly, until then please feel free to rest and take some refreshments. Tealia, I know how you admire my library, take any book you like. We will reconvene soon enough, the rulers from the lower regions will also be joining us as I have called for a meeting."

He turned to Kara and held out his arm. "Will you walk with me daughter."

Kara looked around, they were in a sprawling garden filled with many ponds, lotus flowers and Ficus trees, the roots of some of the trees grew up the trunks giving impressions of wise and ancient faces sculpted into the barks. Other trees entwined with each other in twisted beautiful embraces.

They walked together feeling a profound sense of peace. Lord Eron listened while Kara told him about Maja, Dajo, her childhood, her friends.

"I am grateful to Maja and Dajo for taking care of you, I would like to meet with them in person one day." Eron's head was bent in thought. "You could have chosen to stay with them you know, but you had the courage to break away, even though they had raised you to believe that seeking independence was outrageous." He chuckled briefly. "You chose to rise above the comfort afforded you. You are a true daughter of Eliada because you refused to settle for less than you are. You have remembered your spirit and I sense you have always had faith in a higher power."

He wrapped an arm around Kara's shoulders. "I am so very proud of you."

Kara revelled in the moment, she felt her heart would burst from happiness, but there was one question burning in the back of her mind.

"Will you tell me about my mother?"

Lord Eron gently turned her to face him. "Your mother's name is Gyanna. She is a Guardian of the Earth." He looked into Kara's eyes. "You look just like her."

"Where is she?"

"She was forced to return to her earthly duties." A shadow momentarily crossed Eron's features. "An earth guardian is forbidden to marry and have children, their sworn duty is to the earth... to protect and care for her. The belief is that once a woman gives birth, her child will become her main focus and so her pledge to the earth will be broken."

"What happened?"

"We met and fell in love," Lord Eron said simply. "As Lord of the Rainbow Realm I may marry and have children, there are no laws prohibiting me."

He gestured to a bench by a tree. The tree was covered in a creeper full of purple flowers which cascaded gracefully from the branches. "This was one of your mother's favourite places."

Kara remembered her vision in Onain as she sat down.

"So we married," Lord Eron sat next to her. "But the earth was in uproar at our union... Gyanna did not want to make any more trouble between our worlds, and so she decided it would be better for everyone, and safer for you Kara, if she returned to her duties on earth."

He took hold of Kara's hand. "Your mother loves you and she left to protect you as well as both our worlds. Gyanna gave great consideration to what was best for the Greater Good. Upon her return to earth she was taken to the furthest end of the planet and is forbidden to venture anywhere near our Realm."

He smiled sadly as he touched Kara's crystal bracelet. "This was my gift to your mother, for not just anyone is granted entrance into our Realm. The people were eventually informed about our secret wedding and that they should know my bride by a bracelet she wore. A bracelet with a crystal from each region allowing her to pass without interference. Your mother is a free spirit who loves to go off alone and explore, which she did often here. Not many from The Realm know that Gyanna is a Guardian of Earth, so she has been somewhat of an enigma to many of them. You can rest assured, however, that she is a strong and loyal woman who is very proud of you and has no regrets."

"She spoke to me in Onain." Kara told her father about the vision.

"Ahh yes." Lord Eron's violet eyes softened. "It seems you have inherited your mother's affinity with water. Sometimes the waters of Onain allow Gyanna and I to communicate as well."

"What do you mean by my mother's affinity with water?"

"Every Guardian of Earth has an affinity with one of the earthly elements." Eron plucked a purple flower from the creeper. "For example, Alyne was rescued by Abellona who is also a Guardian of Earth. Abellona has an affinity with the element of fire, because Alyne is from Alfsol she carries the power and protection of the sun within her... a link she shares with the fire elementals of earth. Abellona was drawn to those rocks where Safiri had left Alyne because of their mutual affinity with the sun."

"So Abellona sensed Alyne was in trouble and was drawn to her because of the Alfsol light?"

"Yes," Eron continued, "but Abellona's primary duty is to protect the earth and so she could not take Alyne under her wing for too long, this is the reason she transformed Alyne into an eagle, for her own protection."

"I think I understand... and you say my mother, Gyanna, has an affinity with water."

"Yes... and it appears you have inherited this affinity." Lord Eron handed her the flower.

"No, I don't think so" Kara shook her head.

"Did you not love the rain on earth? Did you not feel strengthened and revived by water?" Eron raised an eyebrow. "Now that you are within The Realm your affinity with water will be enhanced... you will find the power comes to you naturally Kara, if you can keep your wits about you... in extreme situations."

He stood up then. "Mark your mother's words and remember your dream." He looked up. "The others have arrived; it is time to make our way back to the palace."

The palace had many large stately rooms filled with beautiful artwork and statues of saints and angels. There was a feeling of reverence and sanctity within the quiet walls.

Lord Eron showed her into a room where people were seated around a large oval marble table. They all rose as Lord Eron and Kara entered the room. Kara recognised Lukey from Sanguinavia, Thorn of Thendra was also there, the high palace ceilings had allowed him adequate space. She was delighted to see Xylia of Faylin Forest with the Princesses of Arencia. Her eyes fell upon Commander Aldridge resting easily with his son and daughter, Shaydon and Alyne. The Sage and Tealia smiled warmly in greeting with Oldwyn and Oldwina at their side.

Kara rushed to embrace Lukey, Xylia and the princesses before Lord Eron called order and everyone seated themselves. Except for Thorn, who stood awkwardly at the side.

"Welcome friends and rulers of The Realm," Lord Eron began. "Blessed days are these at the return of our children."

Everyone clapped and cheered but Lord Eron silenced them quickly. "However, these wonderful reunions are marred by the return of darker beings as well. Before we can properly celebrate our children's return, we are called to attend to the threat on our precious Realm."

He scanned the faces around the table. "Each region of our Rainbow Realm is highly valuable and essential in maintaining the intricate balance of our world. The Realm's survival depends on the unity and interdependence between our regions. Our security is rooted in Sanguinavia, where our Realm is grounded and connected to our neighbour Earth. In Arencia we celebrate our vitality, and value the need for pleasure to create balance. Alfsol takes ownership of the power within The Realm. It defends and protects our Realm, yet paradoxically, our great warriors are endowed with serenity, gentleness and patience."

He nodded respectfully to Aldridge. "They are confident and not easily threatened." He faced The Sage and bowed. "A different, but more profound power is found in the open hearts of Evergreen, where lies the most compelling energy of the universe… love."

Lord Eron paused before looking to the elders. "We seek our truth in Alverdene and practice the art of communication and negotiation. In Onain we may be offered the gift of sight beyond what our natural eyes can see. If we are allowed this privilege, we should always find the beauty in what is presented to us."

He spread his arms wide. "All of The Realm's energies are shared here in Eliada which is our link to the higher powers. If any one of our regions is under threat our whole world becomes unbalanced and suffers as a consequence. We are called to stand together… and fight this enemy who lurks in our Realm."

Oldwyn stood up to speak. "Because our beautiful Realm is harmonious and balanced, many other beings have lusted after it, we are a bridge of light to powerful worlds beyond and many would take our Realm if they could." He leaned forward on the marble table. "A darkness has been building silently, unbeknownst to us. In the quiet unguarded areas of our Realm dark plots have been developing."

"It all started with Narcissa." Oldwina proceeded to tell them of the vision of Narcissa's heritage and transformation.

The Sage spoke. "She came here with the motive to take our world, becoming pregnant with Safiri was not part of her plan and she saw her son as a burden at first." His voice became compassionate. "Safiri's formative years were dark and dismal because Narcissa was an untrustworthy erratic mother and his father raised him with cold, austere detachment. He grew up fearing rejection, disapproval and abandonment. Eventually he learnt to shut down his feelings, lying and cheating became a way of life for him and a way to earn his mother's approval. As he grew and laid claim to the Alfsol power within him he began to overcompensate for the powerlessness he had felt as a child. He became intimidating, overbearing and aggressive... his ambition now overtakes his mother's. Our Realm holds a key position as a bridge within the universe. His end goal lies further than our Realm."

"We have discovered that he has also inherited the dark powers of the Themians which together with his Alfsol powers have made him a formidable enemy." Oldwina looked across the table at Melia. "The Themians are known for manipulation and deceit, traits Safiri has developed and mastered."

Melia kept her eyes downcast and said nothing.

"Narcissa's personal characteristics of self-entitlement, exclusivity and superiority have also been passed down to Safiri." Lord Eron said. "He truly feels entitled to our Realm and beyond, thinking himself superior to the forces within our universe. We have a duty, not only to protect our Realm, but to block him and his Dark Ones from gaining further access into the universe. He does not appreciate that he has only managed to get thus far due to his alliance with Fergus."

"Yes, we also made the mistake in not paying too much attention to Fergus." Oldwyn nodded regretfully. "His kind have been keeper to various Realm portals across the universe since the beginning of time. Who would have thought Fergus capable of such treachery? Truth be told, we hardly gave thought to him at all, we had all known him for eons, there was no reason to distrust him and we took him for granted."

"Indifference and neglect are often the root of so many evils." Eron agreed sombrely. "Perhaps Safiri, in his arrogance, will make the same mistake as we did with Fergus."

"When the portal closed, we took to Onain seeking answers. Fergus was one step ahead of us," continued Oldwyn. "Due to his unique magical powers he had remained hidden in The Realm undetected. He infected the waters of Onain with a potion of lies that he had concocted, obscuring the reality of the actual events and feeding us with disillusions. We wondered at the murkiness of the waters for many moons but believed what we saw, which was Fergus being overpowered by Dark Ones all those years ago and his Keeper abilities being stolen from him by the Themians before he was blasted far away on earth. Obviously, this was a complete fabrication, cleverly constructed by Fergus. However, the truth shall always prevail and we have discovered that he was using his invisibility and that dreadful mask of deceit within The Realm to hide, impersonate and silently create portals and tunnels for our enemies these past years."

"These portals can only be accessed within the regions and only by those with teleporting abilities, hence the need for the additional tunnels allowing the rest of the Dark Army movement." Lord Eron drummed his fingers on the table, "Fergus was just as trapped as all of us with the closing of the main portal. But he bided his time, as I did, knowing the portal had to open eventually, once it re-opened, he made his way straight back to earth and Safiri with the mask of Deceit."

Eron looked to Xylia. "Recently the mask was being used by a Themian placed at the Gate. Fergus bestowed his Keeping powers temporarily on the Themian who was then able to give access to Safiri's army, even though this army was defeated at Alfsol, still more enemies have been infiltrating secretly, slithering in undetected…"

Xylia stood up abruptly. "We have taken care of this problem." She flung the hideous mask on the table.

The mask was grotesque and looked like it had been burned and melted in places. Many people shuddered at the look of it. Kara noticed that Melia was most visibly shaken.

"We do not know how long the Themian held the gate, for he was disguised as Fergus," continued Xylia, "but when we received the message from Alverdene, the Faylin Forest creatures captured him at once… he has been imprisoned."

Thorn bowed awkwardly before them. "For now, Lord Eron has temporarily bestowed our Thendra the powers to act as keepers to the gate. We Thendra have undertaken to work with Faylin Forest to keep the Rainbow portal safe until a permanent replacement for Keeper of the Gate is employed."

"Our deepest gratitude goes to Xylia and Faylin, our most trusted allies." Eron placed his hand to his heart and bowed to Xylia before turning to Thorn. "Thendra have always had our love, respect and trust. Your kind are our world's treasure, I know the portal will be safe now, we are blessed to have Thendra act as keepers to the gate, I intend to make this a permanent arrangement once I have universal approval."

"Some of Safiri's creatures infiltrated our mines recently." Master Lukey could not keep quiet any longer. "It comes as no surprise to me that Fergus has had his beady eyes on our precious gems for sure, for sure!"

"We are aware that Themians were placed in the mines to cause havoc and discord between the miners." Eron said. "The mines are where the tunnels were created."

"I was forced to shut down the mines before a murder took place, yes murder, I've never seen my kind turned so violently against each other, I would never have thought it, never." Lukey shook his head angrily.

"I have sent Alfsol warriors down to Sanguinavia." Aldridge stood up. "Our scouts inform us that there are still Themians in the area."

"Due to their ability to teleport within The Realm between the portals that Fergus has created, it will be a challenge for you to capture them," stated Lord Eron. "But our advantage is that very few Themians remain, they are close to extinct now. We intend to do the universe a service by eradicating the remaining ones." His lips tightened uncharacteristically. "I expect there is an area within the Ficus Forest they will be gaining access to at any time. But their numbers are few. Their ultimate goal is to free the prisoners of The Purge in the hopes to form an army of the convicts… thus defeating our people and taking The Realm for themselves."

"You are the only person, Lord Eron, who can open the passage to The Purge, how do they mean to capture you?" Alyne asked.

Lord Eron smiled at Alyne before looking to Kara. "By using my daughter," he said simply. "Their plan has always been to get me to sacrifice myself in exchange for Kara's freedom. At first, they only wanted The Realm, but if I am dead, The Purge becomes vulnerable to the powers of Fergus, making them a deadly force beyond The Realm."

Nobody spoke for several moments until Jarita, the copper eagle from Arencia flew noisily into the quiet meeting room and perched on Melia's shoulder, feathers ruffled.

Melia's eyes widened as she listened to Jarita. "Safiri is in the Ficus Forest, he is not alone."

"The time has come." Lord Eron stood up. "Time to put this plot to rest once and for all."

Just then, a bald monk in purple robes knocked urgently at the door, he entered the room and hurried over to Lord Eron and spoke quietly in his ear.

Eron listened and nodded while a slight frown marred his brow. "Rulers of Rainbow Realm." He announced, "it would seem that large parts of Sanguinavia and Arencia have been taken hostage by the Dark Ones within the past hour or so."

"What!" Aurora cried in alarm.

"Let us return at once, immediately!" Lukey roared, slamming his fist on the table.

Lord Eron raised his hands quietening the room. "I must ask you all to remain calm. Safiri and Fergus are requesting an audience with us in Ficus Forest. They play a game of cat and mouse."

Everyone started to protest in outrage.

"With the exception of Commander Aldridge," Eron raised his voice slightly and the room became quiet again. "I request all leaders to accompany me. Aldridge and Shaydon, I must ask you to stay here with Alyne, Tealia and Kara as an extra precaution. The palace is protected but I will feel better knowing that you warriors remain here. If anything should go awry in the forest, we will need the Commander of Alfsol on standby."

"What about Thorn and I?" Xylia went to stand by Thorn.

Lord Eron paused for a moment. "You must accompany us." He turned to Aldridge. "I leave you in charge Sir, until we return."

Chapter Eleven

Safiri

They all followed Lord Eron into the palace's sprawling gardens.

Once outside Eron turned again to Aldridge. "Commander you are needed here. Watch over our loved ones. Guard them with your life. I trust nobody more than you and Shaydon with this responsibility."

He then touched Kara's cheek briefly before he and the other rulers teleported out of sight.

No sooner had they disappeared than the sky turned dark, a smell of burning wood filled the air and a cruel hard laugh was heard. They turned around to see Safiri descending the palace steps.

"One has to question the wisdom and decision making of the 'mighty Lord Eron.' " Safiri made air quotation marks before flicking a small bug from his shoulder. "I personally feel he has gone soft in the head and is no longer competent to rule."

Everyone stared in disbelief and, with the exception of Tealia, they all drew their swords. Safiri expanded slightly but did not retaliate, he put one hand up casually. "Think about it. He left you all here, vulnerable, but none of you has to die. Join me... if you work with me you will be duly rewarded... Eron's Realm as you know it will crumble, but you don't need to crumble with him. It would be wasteful of such talent if you fell because of him."

"Never!" Shouted Shaydon as he and Aldridge charged forward.

Safiri had been expecting this and he swiftly drew his sword. Father and son knocked him off balance but Safiri rolled down the stairs, leapt to his feet and grabbed Kara by her hair in one swift motion. Holding her forcefully by the back of her head he goaded them.

"Not too late to change your minds." With the sword in his other hand he pressed the blade across her throat. *"IT WON'T BE LONG NOW MOTHER!"* he yelled triumphantly into the air.

Kara felt the sword breaking her skin, she could not breathe and she began to sweat profusely. She didn't know if it was from the adrenaline coursing through her or from the extreme heat of Safiri's body. Aldridge and Shaydon looked on terrified. Suddenly a large golden eagle bore down from above, digging its talons into Safiri's face and beating him about the head with its wings. As Safiri released Kara she forcefully jabbed her elbow back into his lower belly and swung around with her sword slicing across his waist, he howled in pain and knocked her down with a swoop of his arm. Momentarily blinded, Kara instinctively rolled out of the way as Shaydon and Aldridge charged at Safiri. She grasped for her sword but it had gone.

She heard Safiri burst into flames and as her sight cleared she saw him expand and tower over Shaydon and Aldridge, she could see the ferocious strokes of all of their swords but the dark smoke and flames obscured a lot of the fight from her.

Aegle landed next to her and transformed immediately back into Alyne. Alyne was choking and gasping, clutching at her own throat. "Too hot!" She wheezed. "The flames... the smoke... it will kill them!" The dagger she usually carried lay on the ground beside her.

"God help us!" Kara called out in despair.

"Kara, call the rain!" Heavenly voices sounded above. Kara looked up to see two brilliant white angels hovering high in the sky. She had never seen anything more glorious and a white heat erupted inside her.

She stood up feeling great power course through her. She knew what she had to do. *"RAIN!"* She yelled, spreading her arms wide open.

Then more commandingly. *"MAKE... IT... RAIN!"*

Thunder exploded and lightening ruptured the sky. Rain burst forth with such violence that the two girls were knocked off their feet.

Kara forced herself up again and pulled Alyne up next to her. She could see Tealia trying to stagger towards them through the torrential downpour.

The battle of swords paused as the heavens opened and Safiri's fire was doused as the rain pounded down hard on all of them. Aldridge had drawn back slightly, wiping the water from his eyes. Although Safiri's fire had been put out he was still almost twice the size of his two opponents. Recovering quickly, he lunged at Shaydon, face contorted in evil rage, red eyes still blazing, he slashed open Shaydon's arm... Shaydon stumbled backwards grasping his arm, Safiri kicked him hard in the chest, knocking him to the ground. Safiri towered over Shaydon with his sword raised in both hands, ready to plunge it down into Shaydon's chest but Aldridge charged at him, yelling fiercely, and rammed his own sword into Safiri's open side knocking him off his feet, Safiri twisted mid fall and slashed his sword across, slicing deeply into Aldridge's chest. Kara and Alyne cried out in horror as Aldridge fell, for he was not wearing any protective armour.

Alyne ran to her father's side while Kara grabbed the dagger from the ground and ran, roaring with rage, at Safiri, blood pounding in her ears. Safiri and Shaydon both leapt to their feet instantly. Safiri swung his sword down at Shaydon but Shaydon dodged to the side and swung around with his sword slashing deeply up and across Safiri's chest. A look of surprise flittered across Safiri's cruel face as Kara leapt up into the air and landed on him piercing him through the side of his neck with the dagger as they fell to the ground.

Kara lay on top of Safiri for several moments , gasping for breath and heart pounding until she felt strong hands lift her up and carry her a short distance, the torrent of rain had calmed down to a soft drizzle. She carefully opened her eyes and looked into her father's concerned face as he laid her down on the bench under the purple cascading flowers. She heard someone cry out loudly in deep pain and anguish and lifted her head to see Shaydon on his knees next to his father, his face twisted in grief and despair as he cried. Kara felt her own heart breaking. While she watched, time seemed to slow, she saw her father and The Sage go to Aldridge and drop to their knees next to his body. The Sage ran his hands over Aldridge's chest and stomach, then shook his head sadly. Lord Eron took Alyne, who was sobbing, into his arms and held her close. She saw Tealia run to Shaydon. Kara tore her eyes away from the tragic scene and saw the rest of the rulers looking on in helpless horror. She saw Melia's eyes widen as they fell on Safiri's still body, the dagger protruding from his neck. Melia moved towards him yelling as she dropped to the ground next to him. Kara could not hear what she was shouting. She saw Safiri raise his head and watched as Melia grabbed the hilt of the protruding dagger and plunge it further into Safiri's gaping wound. His head dropped back to the ground. Kara began to shiver violently and it felt like ice ran through her veins, gripping at her organs. Oldwina approached her carrying a warm purple cloak which she wrapped around Kara's shoulders tightly… and firmly led her away into the palace.

∝ひ♀

Kara could not remember how she had come to be in the softly lit bedroom she found herself in. It was dark outside and she could hear gentle rain falling. Lord Eron came to her side as she woke.

"How are you feeling?" He felt her forehead.

"I'm okay." She croaked; her mouth was dry.

"Here, drink this." Eron handed her a glass of water. Kara felt him watching her closely as she drained the glass.

She remembered seeing Aldridge fall and a sharp pain stabbed at her heart.

"Where are Shaydon and Alyne?"

"They have returned with The Sage and Tealia to Evergreen, they have gone to tell their mother face to face."

"Shaydon was injured?"

"Shaydon was wounded quite badly but will be fine. The Sage has already treated his battle wounds... the wounds of the heart, however, will need more time to heal."

"I want to go to them." She sat up.

"You will, but please, rest now." Eron sat on the side of her bed. "They will be alright in time, they have each other to lean on, and Evergreen is where they need to be right now"

"Where is Safiri?" Panic struck her.

"Safiri is dead... and The Realm is indebted to you and your friends." Eron smiled sadly.

"We killed him?" Kara shook her head in disbelief. "He's gone?"

"He's gone," Eron affirmed. "I believe you struck the final blow and Melia ensured that he will never rise again."

Kara felt numb, she dropped back on her pillow, she could not process anything in that moment. "It's over?" she asked feebly.

"Almost."

She sat up again abruptly remembering..."Alyne... Alyne transformed back into Aegle! She saved me!"

"Yes, she did indeed. You are not the only one with magical powers it seems." Eron smiled as he looked out at the gentle rain falling beyond the window.

"But did she know that she could transform, can she transform at any time?"

"She was not aware, no. It is indeed a rare talent she has been gifted. I saw it in her when we met in Ficus Forest but I knew it would take a crisis to make her aware of it herself… Alyne has been an eagle for more years than she has been herself, now Aegle is part of her, they are one and the same and she will be able to change at will."

"How awesome." Kara smiled in spite of everything. "What happened in the forest?"

"The cunning and disloyal Fergus underestimated us." Eron poured himself a glass of water. "When he was siphoning in Dark Ones and similar beings through the tunnels created in the dwarf mines, he assumed we would be at a disadvantage because we are a Realm of light and are not accustomed to dark energy, he believed we rulers would fall before hundreds of Dark Ones without the light of the Alfsol warriors to protect us. He knows we are bound by honour and rules and when they called for the meeting in the forest, he believed we would be unprepared for the ambush."

He sipped thoughtfully, "The instant we landed in the forest, the Dark Ones attacked us. Their force was great and Master Lukey and the princesses fell. The Elders were weakened but did not fall. Fergus had foolishly forgotten about the mighty powers of Love and Faith. The Sage and I quickly reminded him. Xylia and Thorn were formidable and together we drove away the Dark Ones. Those beings that could be captured were… as was Fergus, who immediately divulged Safiri's location to us. Fergus will suffer the most punishment of them all as his betrayal has been the greatest. He has many crimes to answer for."

Grimacing he put his glass on the table. "They have been imprisoned in The Purge."

"You said Lukey and the princesses fell?"

"Yes, but The Sage quickly revived them. They are more susceptible to the Dark Ones, because they are from the lower regions which are closer to earth."

"Do the Dark Ones roam about the earth freely then?"

"Yes, they do, and unfortunately they cannot be captured, only dispelled. They gravitate towards feelings of fear and doubt which are abundant on planets like earth. Our Realm is of a lighter dimension than earth and all magical powers are enhanced here, whether used for good or bad, which is why it holds such an attraction as well as being a bridge to worlds beyond. Remember this Kara, wherever you may travel, light will always be stronger than dark. Fergus had forgotten it."

"How did Safiri get into the palace?"

"Fergus must have created an illegal portal into the palace many years ago, which enabled Safiri to kidnap you as a baby." Eron shook his head. "The audacity of Fergus. He held a position of utmost honour and his deception cuts deep."

"But ultimately they have failed," Kara took her father's hand, "because light is always stronger than darkness."

Eron smiled "Yes indeed," he agreed, squeezing her hand. "Safiri must have got the shock of his life when Alyne transformed into an eagle and you opened the heavens on him. He greatly underestimated you young women," his smile faded, "he was obviously unprepared for the strength and skills of father and son as well or he would not have dared to come alone."

"I can't believe we have lost Commander Aldridge." Kara said sadly.

"His last days were his happiest, he was reunited with his wife and family, all he had wished for these closed years."

"It seems so unfair. They were taken away from him for so long, and then he had such a short time with them when they finally returned."

"He has died an honourable death, protecting his children and his Realm, he will go into the afterlife a hero. He will have no regrets."

They sat silently for a while listening to the rain pattering against the window.

"What of Sanguinavia and Arencia?" Kara asked. "They were taken by the Dark Ones."

"Sanguinavia and Arencia are no longer under siege. Now that their masters have been defeated the Dark Ones have drifted away. There are a few Themians who have scattered but they will not last long, their powers are mostly diminished at this stage. They need to sacrifice each other to grow in power and there are too few of them to do so. The Themians are as good as finished. The elders and I will begin the work of cleansing the tunnels and finding the illegitimate portals. A lot of love and light will be needed to clear away the psychic debris, but we will ensure peace and harmony is restored throughout The Realm."

They were quiet for several moments again, the sound of the rain was lulling Kara back to sleep, her eyelids felt heavy, she strained to keep them open but could not, she heard her father say.

"Sleep now Kara, everything will be alright, you are home." She felt him pull the covers over her and kiss her forehead lightly before sleep pulled her away into dreams of angels.

Chapter Twelve

The End of This Journey

Kara slept late into the next morning. Lord Eron eventually woke her suggesting a picnic brunch near the Eryl lagoon. Violet and silver robes were brought for her to wear. They walked through the tranquil city of Eliada admiring its beautiful buildings. There were a lot of priestly and monk-like folk about as well as happy families and children strolling around the serene cobbled streets and green parks or resting by the many ponds and fountains that could be found throughout the holy city. The people all wore peaceful angelic expressions and stopped to introduce themselves and welcome Kara home. Lord Eron acknowledged all they passed and beamed proudly over Kara. He knew everyone by name and Kara could see how loved and respected he was by all.

After a while he turned to Kara. "You will have plenty of time to explore our city and meet the wonderful people and families here, but I am very hungry, aren't you? Shall we teleport to Eryl Lagoon? A picnic has been prepared there for us." He held out his hand which Kara took. She enjoyed the spinning sensation as they swirled in the vortex of air. They landed smoothly by a beautiful lagoon nestled in amongst scenic surroundings of lush greenery with a backdrop of snow-capped mountains. The Eliada skies were a soft lilac hue.

A large picnic blanket was laid out with an enormous basket beside it. Eron unpacked an assortment of breads, honeyed fruits and other delicacies. They sat and appreciated the beautiful setting, the food and being alone together at last. However, Kara's thoughts kept returning to her friends, Aldridge and the angels who had called down to her. She asked her father about the angels.

"Angels are commonly sighted here in Eliada." Eron looked up at the sky. "Although you may sometimes feel as if you are alone in life's journey, you truly are never alone, wherever you may be, you can always ask God for help at any time, in quiet times or moments of crisis and He will answer, sometimes by sending His angels."

"Why didn't the angels save Aldridge?"

"Angels will not interfere if it is a person's time to die. Death is just another path that some may take. Here in The Realm some are immortal, but it is not promised, death is not the end it is but another journey."

Kara looked into the calm waters of the lagoon thoughtfully.

"I find this lagoon calms life's ripples." Her father spoke gently. "Eliada is a city built on true faith. And when you experience true faith in higher powers your life will shift from survival... to infinite possibility."

"How safe is The Purge?" Kara changed the subject. "We have underestimated Fergus before, should we not destroy him and be done with this all?"

"Prisoners are stripped of all magical powers when incarcerated in The Purge." Eron stood up. "However, he will still have his wits as Narcissa does. And they both possess very sharp wits. I will meet with my councillors shortly to pass judgement on the appropriate punishments for Fergus. One always has to keep in mind that the very person we wish to destroy may yet have a larger role to play in our future."

He rose and walked to the water's edge.

Kara followed him. "There are so many lotus flowers here in Eliada. I see them everywhere." She gazed at the beautiful flowers that seemed to float on top of the water.

"They are my favorite of all flowers." Eron wrapped his arm around Kara's shoulders. "Because they are symbolic of purity and spiritual enlightenment, emerging from the mud with beauty and grace. Their unfolding petals suggest expansion of the soul."

"I feel like I have so much to prove here." Kara blurted out. "Like so much is expected of me."

"Kara… you have just defeated a great evil. You will be famous for this great feat, regardless of being my daughter. Remember it does not matter what you were born, but what you grow to be. Every being at some stage has to choose between what is right and what is easy… and it is our choices that show who we truly are more than our abilities… or our heritage." Eron kissed her cheek. "I would be in awe of you whether you were my daughter or not."

Kara rested her head on her father's shoulder. "You're right. I do feel like anything is possible here in Eliada."

"That's the spirit." Eron chuckled softly. He waved his hand over the water and an image of a rainbow appeared on its smooth surface. "Each individual contains energy centres within them which are likened to our regions within the Rainbow Realm, see how spiritual balance is achieved every time we ground ourselves into our body and provide for our survival… every time we celebrate our vitality, sensuality and nurture our emotions … every time we take ownership of our power, our will and personal sovereignty."

As he spoke images of Sanguinavia, Arencia and Alfsol were reflected on the clear waters of the lagoon. "Every time we open our heart to give and receive love… every time we use our creative expression to speak our truth and every time we use our perception and psychic awareness to see what lies beyond appearances."

Images of Evergreen, Alverdene and Onain drifted across the surface. Eron turned to smile at Kara as the reflection of Eliada finally graced the waters.

"And every time we connect with our Creator and allow ourselves to be spiritually guided."

A loud roar came from the mountains and they watched as a stunning golden dragon came into sight. Soaring high into the clouds and dipping low below the mountain peaks.

"Drakontus," Kara whispered.

"Our Commander in Chief will be memorialised tomorrow in Alfsol." Eron watched the dragon. "Drakontus has been released in his honour."

❧

It was a beautiful ceremony. The Alfsol warriors sent their Commander in Chief off to the sound of beating drums and the trumpet of triumph and glory, while Drakontus soared and dipped around the blazing skies of Alfsol. All the leaders from the seven regions were in attendance.

Xylia was also there translucent yet powerful. Kara heard Xylia's voice in her mind. "*You have accomplished much Kara Gabriel, in such a short time, you have surpassed even my expectations of you. Perhaps those who are best suited to power are those who have never sought it.*"

Mystique the unicorn stood majestically at Xylia's side for most of the service before he eventually moved away to stand between The Sage and Tealia, nudging them gently.

The Sage, the Elders and Lord Eron all gave honourable eulogies for their worthy Commander in Chief and when Shaydon finally spoke Kara broke down in tears and could not hear anything he said. Aurora and Melia came to her side to comfort her.

"Don't worry," Aurora whispered. "Shaydon is going to be fine, he has grown so much and so have you."

Melia embraced Kara tightly "Aldridge will live on in legends. The defeat of Safiri will go down in history."

Thorn stood in a cluster of equally tall and awkward Thendra together with Master Lukey and several dwarves representing Sanguinavia. Lukey cried unashamedly and blew his nose loudly several times.

Alyne stood tall by her mother's side holding her up throughout the service. Kit and Len stood protectively on either side of mother and daughter.

Sometime after the service Shaydon pulled Kara gently aside and asked her to go for a walk with him. Clouds had covered the sun and the weather had cooled. They strolled through a field of sunflowers.

"I'm so sorry Shaydon, it is unfair that you have lost your father so soon after reuniting with him. You have been robbed."

"No, those few days I had with my father were a gift." Shaydon smiled sadly. "Everything that needed to be said was said. I had carried so much guilt about what happened to my mother and Alyne, but my father absolved me. We experienced the invasion together and were torn apart because of it... but we did not cause the invasion... we both responded to it in the best way we knew how at the time. My father assured me that he felt nothing but love and pride for me and I will always treasure the short time we had together, we were closer in those few days than we ever were before."

Kara squeezed his arm sympathetically. "Is your mother going to be ok?" she asked.

"My mother is stronger now than she was before. She is yet to tell us about the dreams she had during her long sleep. She was on her own life changing journey. Her and my father made the most of every moment they had together. They learnt that life can change in an instant and

171

tomorrow is not promised." Shaydon ran his hand through the sunflower stems as they walked.

"I know it looks like Alyne is being strong for her now but mother knows Alyne will need her guidance and support before long. Alyne is still lost. My father's death will be harder on her than the rest of us."

They walked on in silence for a few moments until Shaydon broke out in a smile. "And, aside from that my mother will want to be around for the birth of her grandchildren."

Kara stopped in her tracks. "What do you mean?"

"I mean to ask Tealia to marry me. Not right now of course, but in due time. My father gave me his blessing and urged me to ask her soon. I know about the visions Tealia saw in Onain... I was blessed with similar visions of us with our three children."

Kara hugged him impulsively. "Oh Shaydon! I'm so happy now I know that you are going to be alright."

"You have come a long way little one... since the day I found you lost and crying in Faylin." Shaydon stepped back keeping hold of her shoulders. "You have grown into a courageous, strong and beautiful young woman and it has been an honour to share your journey with you."

"Thank you Shaydon, for everything you have done for me. For always being there and for bringing me home. I can't imagine my life without you."

"I will always be here for you Kara. We fought side by side and conquered Safiri." Shaydon smiled. "Somehow I don't think it was an accident on Lord Eron's part. I think he meant for us to face Safiri and defeat him."

"He took a big risk if that's true." Kara frowned pushing her hair back. "Leaving us to deal with Safiri, what if we had failed?"

"Your father had faith in us and faith can move mountains."

"What happens now?"

"The next chapter of our lives begins now Kara. I know you are ready for it. I get the feeling there are a few more adventures for us in the future." Shaydon wrapped his arm around Kara's shoulder and they both looked up at the luminescent rainbow that had appeared in the sky. A beautiful golden eagle glided freely through it.

Glossary

Kara Gabriel	Our teenage heroine
Maja and Dajo	Kara's foster parents on earth
Shaydon	Kara's best friend and loyal protector
Aegle	Shaydon's beloved eagle
Faylin Forest	Enchanted boarder between earth and The Realm
Xylia	Fierce protector and guardian of Faylin Forest
Fergus	Keeper of the Gate. Guard to the main portal between earth and The Realm

The Rainbow Realm known as:

The Realm	A small world made up of seven regions. It is a bridge between earth and other worlds.
Sanguinavia	**Region of Supply** Home to the red dwarves and the dwarf mines. Sanguinavia supplies all types of produce to The Realm. It is considered to be the foundation of The Realm.

Master Lukey	Governor of Sanguinavia
The Red Wood	Boarder between the main portal and Sanguinavia
Thendra	Thendron (single) Thendra (plural). Tree folk. Guardians of The Red Wood.
Thorn	A Thendron, he is the main 'spokesperson' for Thendra.
Arencia	**Region of Pleasure and Vitality**
Princess Aurora	Princess of Arencia
Princess Melia	Princess of Arencia. Younger sister to Aurora.
Jarita	Copper eagle mascot and messenger of Arencia
Alfsol	**Region of Defense** Home to Alfsol warriors, defenders of The Realm
Commander Caine	Former commander of Alfsol.
Narcissa	Wife to Commander Caine.
Commander Aldridge	Current Commander of Alfsol. Father to Shaydon
Alyne	Sister to Shaydon Daughter to Aldridge
Kit and Len	Sisters to Aldridge Aunts to Shaydon and Alyne
Evergreen	**Region of Love and Healing**
The Sage	Steward of Evergreen and

	Advisor to Lord Eron
Tealia	Daughter to The Sage
Katran	Wife to Commander Aldridge of Alfsol
	Mother to Shaydon and Alyne
The Cerulean Forest	Bordering forest between the regions of Evergreen and Alverdene

Alverdene	**Region of Communications**
	Home to the Elders
Oldwina	Guardian of Alverdene
	Adviser to Lord Eron
Oldwyn	Guardian of Alverdene
	Adviser to Lord Eron

| **Onain** | **Region of Vision** |
| **Garden of Illumination** | The enchanted garden of Onain where some may be granted visions of the past or the future as well as insights into present situations |

Eliada	**Capital Region of The Realm**
	Region of Faith
Lord Eron	Governor of Eliada
	Ruler of The Realm
	Father to Kara Gabriel
Eryl Lagoon	Outskirts of Eliada
Ficus Forest	A place for meditation on the outskirts of Eliada

The Purge.   Prison of The Realm

Safiri.   Evil enemy of Kara and
                        The Realm
                        Son to Commander Caine of
                        Alfsol and Narcissa
Themians   Nasty troublemakers and enemies
                        of The Realm
Slyne   Leader of the Themians
Dark Ones.   Evil faceless creatures
                        Enemies of mankind and
                        The Realm

About the Author

Katrina has been an avid fan of classic fantasy and spirituality readings. She recognises the importance of using one's own efforts and resources to achieve objectives, and that life's circumstances and incidents are the basis of learning about self-reliance and building resilience. As the mother of three young adults she was inspired to create this entertaining fantasy which reflects her ideals and the ethos of her life. She currently resides in Zambia, Africa.